Empires of Dust

A Novel
By William Monroe

To my creative writing teacher Jim

[signature]

Act I: Chapter 1: Nowhere Again

The windshield wipers beat lazily as little Lily DuCray sat alone in the passenger seat of her Mom's silver Toyota Camry outside the clinic. She squirmed uncomfortably as she waited in her jeans and pink *My Little Pony* t-shirt bearing the purple cartoon pony with plastic gem studded rainbow mane and big eyes with thick lashes. She stared fixedly through the window at the activity inside the little emergency room at the Fallbrook Clinic.

The figures in white lab coats and blue scrubs seemed as insubstantial as ghosts flitting around the bed. The bloated, blue tinged, bare chested man on the bed she saw with horrid clarity as he arched his back convulsively and collapsed back again.

"It can't be him," she thought. "That can't be my Dad! He is always happy and full of warm smiles, nothing like the twisted man grimacing on the hospital bed."

She got out of the car and went around the wing of the squat building to the wide glass doors with the big red letters EMERGENCY on the white plastic sign above them. The two sets of glass double doors slid wide at her approach and she turned past the unmanned reception window toward the big double doors of the trauma center. Then she heard her mother wail, and the shouting started. She turned and fled back into the rain.

Lily woke groggily, the sound of yelling from the living room down the hall beyond her bedroom door blending with the yelling in her bad dream. She rolled to her back, eyes open wide in the dark as she heard her door click shut. "Ben!" she thought, "He was in my room again! Damn him and his Father and this whole town!"

"You'll do what I fucking tell you to do," shouted her stepfather angrily, "and you better fucking wipe that pathetic frown off your face or I will." A crash and a thud sounded and he said, "Clean up this fucking mess!"

Heavy footsteps thumped down the hall, her door slammed open, and light from the hall flashed upon her face and rigid form below the covers. The big man's shadowy silhouette blotted out the light and cast her into darkness again.

"Get your ass to sleep before I have to knock the shit outa you!" he roared. "You cause nothing but trouble for me and Ben, when we welcome you in our fucking house. One more fucking word about Ben to your whiny Mother or that fucking counselor and you'll be fucking sorry!"

The door slammed shut to leave her crying in the silent darkness for many long hours before she drifted back to sleep.

Chapter 2: We Don't Do That Around Here

She woke slowly to the blaring beep of her old alarm clock, slapping it into silence with a few clumsy swats as she struggled to wake. She sat and rubbed at her eyes with the palm of her hands. Then she swung her feet off the bed and crept to the door, turning the knob and peeking into the hall. Seeing the bathroom door ajar, she darted across the hall into the bathroom and closed and latched it behind her.

When she finished her biological business, she showered, brushed her teeth, and put her long hair into a ponytail before returning to her room. She dug through the small assembly of outdated clothing in her little closet, selecting the pair of jeans that seemed to fit her lean body best, along with the old, tight, threadbare *My Little Pony* t-shirt.

The kitchen, too, was unoccupied, so she ate a bowl of *Toasty Ohs* and drank a bit of lukewarm coffee before turning out the horses and beginning the two-mile walk to school. Neither her Mom's old Camry, Jake's aging blue Ford pickup, nor Ben's red Dodge were in the yard.

Several times she saw classmates whiz by in their own cars or with parents or friends as she walked along the roadside, but she did not lift her thumb to ask for a ride, nor did any of the vehicles slow to offer.

She rubbed her bloodshot eyes as she walked through the parking lot filled with aging pickup trucks and a few newer cars and SUVs. There was Ben's big truck, in the corner of the lot by the football field, a big red Dodge with oversized tires and a lift kit, chrome roll bars with lights and a cowcatcher.

She hung her head and tried not to see the small crowd hanging around by the truck, walking quicker toward the wide doors to the school.

"Have a nice walk?" said Ben loudly from the group around the truck. A few laughs followed. She did not look over at the mocking faces and Ben continued, "Where's your sense of humor? That shitty California attitude will get you nowhere."

From the corner of her eye she saw that Ben and his posse were moving on an intercept course toward the school doors so she gripped her stack of books and notebooks tighter and hurried forward. Too late, she saw as Ben rushed to the doors, pulling one side wide and holding it for her as she came to it. As she stepped through he swung the heavy door into her, knocking her books from her grip and slamming her into the other door. "Oops." he said, "too slow, lost my grip."

She stooped to pick up her books and papers, some of which were caught beneath the door and were crumpled and scraped against the concrete sidewalk. "Let me help you with that." said Ben bending to rip her drawing notebook from below the door and hold up its mangled pages.

"What is this shit?" The page displayed was a finely rendered drawing of a bare breasted mermaid beckoning to a besotted sailor in a dinghy. "Look at this shit!" said Ben. "You sure are a pervert for such a prude. We don't draw shit like that around here." He stuffed the torn page into his jacket pocket and said, "You best get a better attitude or the Principle is gonna see the shit you draw."

Then Ben let go of the door again and it scraped the remaining books and papers and bumped Lily off balance to land on her ass on the concrete in the doorway. Ben laughed again and continued into the building, his entourage pushing Lily aside and stepping on the papers as they followed.

Lily hurriedly gathered her books and papers as the bell rang, and she rushed in late to her classroom to take her seat. The Teacher, Mrs. Sanderson, glared at her over her reading glasses, and a few of her classmates chuckled while Lily tried to quietly reorganize her scrambled papers and find her place in the lesson book.

"Please let me just make it through today without any more disasters." she thought to herself as Mrs. Sanderson resumed her lesson, some ridiculous point about Manifest Destiny and the settlement of the Americas. "I'm afraid it's my Manifest Destiny to have a very bad day."

Still her frequent nightmare was fresh in her mind, and a poem came to her mind, so she jotted it down in her little notebook journal:

Headlights revealing a world without end.
Driving on forever, each destination sends me onward
To arrive at Nowhere again.
Hasty medics, electrostats and wires
His fat form bloated, arching.
His fleshy face turns blue with death,
And somewhere nearby, the swinging of the scythe.
Headlights revealing a world without end.
Driving on forever, each destination sends me onward
To arrive at Nowhere Again

With a start she looked up to see Mrs. Sanderson standing beside her desk, staring down over her pointy nose at Lily. Lily blinked a couple of times as she noticed her own tears welling in her shiny eyes.

Mrs. Sanderson snatched the notebook from its hiding place in the lesson book. "We are here to study American History," she said, "not scribble inane verse. You are a deeply disturbed girl, Miss Ducray."

Sure enough, a few minutes later the Principle, Mr. Meadows stepped through the classroom door in his blue shirt, brown jacket and shoes, and grey pants. He looked at her sternly, saying "Lily DuCray, I need you to come to my office."

A couple of girls giggled at that, and the teacher glared at both Lily and the girls as Lily rose and gathered her abused books, hurrying to the Principal as he waited holding open the door. Mrs. Sanderson handed Lily's little journal to the Principal with a frown and sad shake of her head as Lily got to the doorway.

They walked briskly down the hall and into the administration wing past the receptionist, who gave Lily the slightest glance before concentrating on her computer screen. They entered the Principal's office, and Mr. Meadows closed the door behind them. He beckoned to a pair of padded chairs in front of his desk before settling heavily into his own big brown faux leather office chair.

"I hear you've been making trouble for your Brother Ben." he said looking at her sternly.

"Stepbrother," said Lily icily, "and he is the one making trouble for me."

Meadows glanced down at some papers on his desk and continued, "Ben has always been a team player. Everyone respects him and he's one of our star football players in his Senior year." He shuffled through the papers, pulling out the torn drawing and a report.

"I can't believe the things you said about Ben to Mrs. Mulder. You have a serious problem, Miss DuCray. You accuse your step brother of sexual misconduct, but then you draw and write stuff like this." He slapped his hand down on the drawing and journal and shoved them forward with a sneer.

"It's called art," spat Lily, "and they teach it in real schools."

"I'm giving you a five-day suspension, starting today." said Mr. Meadows flatly. He looked up from the papers and continued, "When you return, you will issue an apology to Ben and Mrs. Mulder for defamation of character and wasting school councilor time."

He paused for dramatic effect, and continued, "You will also help set up for the Sadie Hawkins dance after school tonight. Its time you learn how to interact with others as part of the team rather than just entertaining your own personal agenda. Now go home and apologize to your parents for being such a nuisance. You are dismissed."

She stood without a word, and turned to open the door without raising her glance to Mr. Meadows. She did not even notice the expression of pity from the Receptionist as she strode to the school doors and pushed them wide, straining to hold back the welling tears.

She walked back home slowly, and made her way to the corral where her Mom kept her horse, Redwing with the Vigil's three horses. As soon as he saw her walking toward the corral, Redwing whickered and ran up to the fence, nuzzling her hand eagerly with his velvety nose.

"What a good boy, Redwing." she said, scratching him gently behind the ears. She kissed his nose and rubbed along his jawline as he nibbled at her hands. "Sorry, no treats right now, honey." She followed the fence-line along the driveway to the gate, pulled the latch chain from the notch, and dragged it through the fence to hang clanking against the gate as she opened it and stepped through.

She re-latched the gate chain and came alongside Redwing, rubbing his smooth summer coat and patting his barrel chest. "Good boy, Redwing." she repeated again and again to a chorus of whickering and funny flapping horse lips.

Then she gripped his mane and swung up onto him bareback. He trotted eagerly the moment she sat forward and kicked her heels gently to his flanks, breaking into a run at her urging. Around and around the corral they ran, and she smiled wide at the thrill of it, perched like a jockey almost kneeling upon his surging back. Finally, she sat back and Redwing slowed to a trot and went toward the barn where he knew the bag of oats awaited.

Just then the slamming of the house door alerted her as her stepfather came out of the house in a visible rage. "Get off that fucking horse!" he yelled. Her Mother followed him out of the house with wide eyes.

She dismounted obediently, plodding toward the gate with Redwing following and nudging her shoulder. She reopened the gate, leaving the corral and re-latching the gate. As she turned back toward the house her stepfather slapped her full across the face and she reeled into the gate.

He stepped up to the gate, grabbing her hair and pulling her up to his red face. Then Redwing bit him hard on the neck and he hollered, releasing her to swing a fist ineffectually at the horse.

"Leave her alone, Jake!" screamed her Mother with teary eyes.

Jake whirled on Lily's Mom, backhanding her across the face and sending her sprawling to her back with a bloody lip. "Get back in the fucking house!" he shouted, looming over her.

Lily's Mom scrambled back and to her feet, retreating toward the house, and Jake turned to Lily again. "Clean out all the stalls, and brush all the horses," he said, "and your Mother and I will decide what to do with you."

Lily watched her Mom walk toward the house with a brief glance back toward Lily. Jake too turned and stomped away, leaving Lily alone with the horses.

Lily spent the day shoveling manure out of the stalls and hauling it by wheelbarrow to the compost pile in the corner of the field. By mid-afternoon she had the stalls clean, so she curried and brushed the horses lovingly. She chatted with them as she worked, and gave each a handful of oats as she finished.

She had started with Redwing, and he whickered and whinnied jealously at the attention given the others. When all the horses' coats were clean and shiny, she climbed into the hayloft and pushed down a bale.

She stretched up and crammed a hand into the pocket of her jeans, pulling out her pocket knife and picking out the folding blade. Then she cut the twine and tossed a flake of hay into each stall before leaving the barn and the contented horses.

She crossed the yard past her Mom's Camry and Jake's Ford, plodding up the steps to the house and slowly opening the door. Her Mother was nowhere to be seen, but Jake lounged on the couch drinking a can of Bud Light with his feet on the coffee table. Fox News blared from the TV, but Jake turned at the sound of her entry.

"Time for you to hike your ass back to school." said Jake. "Principal's office called and said you need to help set up for the School Dance and learn how to play well with others. Maybe you can learn to act like a normal girl. Get going, your Mom and I have things to discuss."

Again, she began the long walk back to the school, this time with her classmates and their parents passing by in their vehicles going the other way. Again, she saw Ben's truck in the corner of the parking lot by the football field, but this time Ben and the team were out on the field for practice and she entered the school alone.

She turned and walked down the hall to the gym where the dance was to be held, pushing the big door open as quietly as possible. Still the five girls at work on the decorations turned as one at her entry.

"Look what the cat dragged in." said Ben's sometimes girlfriend Katie Mallory as Lily walked in. "It's the Lily of the Valley Girls here slumming with the hicks."

The other girls giggled, and Katie sneered at Lily with a mocking smile that twisted her pretty face in its frame of stylish blonde hair.

"We'd have you help with the decorations," chimed in Sarah Marshall, "but we don't know what kind of perverted stuff you might draw on the banners."

The girls laughed again and Lily stared at them coldly for a moment before turning away to look around the hall. A bearded twenty-something man worked on the sound system at the far end of the room, pointedly ignoring the conversation between the girls. A table had been set with several turntables, a rack of amplifiers and other equipment, and a pair of big speakers sat on stands to either side near the walls.

She walked tentatively over to him, and he looked up with a little smile. "Can I give you a hand?" she asked as confidently as she could.

He beamed at her at the invitation and his glance made her keenly aware of how tight her outgrown shirt was over her swelling breasts and hardening nipples.

"Sure!" he said with an effort not to sound too eager. "Come on over here and I'll show you what we've got going on."

She blushed and walked the rest of the way to him.

"We've got to run this power cable over to the Subwoofer along the back wall," he said holding up the end of a cable. He handed her the cable end and pointed to the subwoofer, continuing "and then we'll need to run speaker cable to the sub and both of the mains."

She glanced down at the coiled cables in the case at his feet before taking the power cable over to the sub and inserting it into the port.

Lily helped with the other cables, and watched and listened as he hooked up the rest of the system. Soon he said "Right on! I think we're ready to give it a try." He smiled at Lily again and said," Got a favorite song you'd like to hear?"

She stared at him with a slightly scared look for a moment and he said, "We can play just about any song you want from the digital library on the net."

"No Doubt!" she said.

"The band, or are you just agreeing with me?" he asked with a chuckle and another smile.

"The band," she replied, "I'm Just a Girl in the World."

"You got it." he said as he lifted his tablet computer, "What's your name, pretty Girl in the World?"

"Lily DuCray." she said, "What's your name, Mr. Sound Man."

"Duane Murphy." he replied, "but tonight I'm DJ Claptrap, playin' your requests and the best tunes old and new."

They smiled at each other with gleaming eyes for a moment before he returned his attention to the tablet. A few seconds later the speakers played out the first notes of the song, and he looked back up at Lily. "I play the tunes, you dance."

She stared at him blankly a moment, and he clarified, "This is a dance we're setting up for, right?"

She nodded mutely, but still stood still.

"Come on!" said Duane, "You definitely look like a girl who can dance." He strode a pace forward and took her hands in his. "I'll even dance if it makes you feel better."

He began to step back and forth, still holding her hands until she began to join in. When they had established a pattern, he let go her hands and did some silly moves, gyrating his hips and prancing about until she laughed aloud and joined in the antics. By the end of the song, both were laughing and reeling, and Lily could barely recall having ever had as much fun. She did not even notice the hateful stares of Katie Mallory or the spiteful derision of the other girls, nor did she see Katie suddenly get up and leave the room.

A few minutes later the gym door flew open and Principal Meadows stormed in, Katie Mallory close at his heels and sneering. The Principal marched straight up to the sound booth where Lily and Duane sat chatting and listening to more music as they adjusted sound settings.

"Lily DuCray, you are banned from this dance." said Meadows, "We do not dance like that around here. We do not allow blatantly sexual booty shaking, or twerking, or whatever in this school."

Lily began to protest, "I wasn't twerking or doing anyth..."

"Get out!" shouted the Principal, interrupting and pointing to the door. "You should be ashamed!"

Duane spoke up, "She wasn't dancing at all inappropriately, Sir, she was just..."

"Miss Mallory already told me what you were 'just' doing," interrupted Meadows again, "and we won't have that sort of behavior in this school. You, 'Sir'," he continued, "will refrain from fraternizing with the students or the Sherriff will be called to escort you off school property."

Duane's jaw dropped and he searched for a response, but Lily just turned and ran out the doors of the gymnasium and all the way home with tears in her eyes.

As she walked toward the house, she saw that both her Mom's car and Jake's truck were gone from the driveway. Relieved at the reprieve from Jake's cruel judgement, she went in the house, poured a glass of water from the tap and plopped onto the sofa. She leaned forward and grabbed the remote, clicking on the TV and browsing channels.

She settled on a suspenseful horror flick with a ghostly girl haunting a family via a VCR tape called *The Ring*. She kicked off her shoes, lay back on the couch, and soon dozed off, weary from the last night's poor rest and the day's hard work and stress.

She ran through the rain, away from the lights and the EMERGENCY sign and the spasming thing which could not be her Dad. She ran and ran and ran, sputtering rain from her gasping wet lips and completely soaked.

It seemed that the light behind her got closer the more she ran, and at last the lights caught up and pulled beside her. She glanced over and saw that the lights were the headlights of her Mom's car.

The window rolled down and her Mom's shadowed silhouette called to her in a choked emotional voice, "Come on, Lily, get in the car before you catch pneumonia."

Her running steps faltered to a stop and the car door swung open. Lily got in, sobbing and shivering wet.

"I'm so sorry, honey." cried her Mom, leaning over tearfully to embrace Lily. "He loved us both very, very much, but it can't be helped."

She burst into tears, pressing her face into her Mother's shoulder and sobbing, "No! It can't be him. That wasn't my Dad."

"Oh, Honey!" called her Mom again, "I'm so sorry. He was just too good for this world, and God called him home."

"No!" Lily screamed, "No, no, no, no!"

Her Mom put her hands on Lily's shoulders and pushed her back to arm's length. "Look at me." she said.

Lily looked up at her Mom, and screamed again incoherently. Her Mom's hair hung sodden down over her face and her flesh moldered and turned a sickly yellow-grey, with pasty black lips grimacing wetly. "I'm so sorry, Honey." repeated her Mother's dead visage.

Chapter 3: Shadow Creep

"Quit your screaming and get off the damn couch," shouted Jake over her faltering screams, "and fix some dinner. Ben will be home from football practice soon, and you better damn well have supper ready by then."

Lily rolled to her feet quickly, wide eyed and startled. "Where's my Mom?" she asked as she looked around desperately.

Jake stared at her coldly, then smiled with a sneer, "She ran off back to California 'cause she's sick of your bullshit."

Lily gasped and glared at him, clenching her fists and jaw. "She would never leave me behind."

"Sure as shit she did." laughed Jake. "Get your shit together and maybe she'll come back." His eyes and jaw hardened, "Now get in the fuckin' kitchen and fix some dinner."

She turned and ran into the kitchen crying again.

She fried up some greasy burgers and onions and made patty melts, minute rice, and canned green beans with teary eyes and panicky movements. Then as Ben came in she darted out the door and ran to the barn.

Redwing snorted as she flung open the barn door and came in, scratching at the floor with a hoof and snorting again when she ran past him and climbed the ladder into the loft. She fell to her face on the hay strewn plank floor and sobbed into her arms for many long moments before rising as a shadow fell across the open doorway to the barn.

Ben stood in the doorway, leaning against the doorframe with arms crossed in front of his red Nike *Just Do It* tee shirt. His tight jeans clung to his muscular legs and showed plainly the bulge of his manhood. "You shouldn't have slapped me for touching you while you were sleeping." said Ben from the doorway. "You should feel lucky anyone wants to touch you at all."

He strode forward along the front of the horse stalls. "Be careful, you'll fall from the loft there. Watch out, you just might break your neck." He paused, looking up at her with a sharp glint in his brown eyes. "Your Mama ain't here to save you this time. Give me what I want, and things will be a lot easier for you."

She glanced around desperately for somewhere to run, but saw the pitchfork leaning against the open stall next to Redwing. She rolled to the edge of the loft, grabbed the upright of the ladder and swung down, landing in a roll toward Redwing's stall. Jumping to her feet she ran to the gate, dropping and rolling beneath it.

Redwing jumped back, backing into the end of the stall, and Ben leapt to the gate, lifting the latch. Lily sprang up, reaching for the fork, but Ben swung the gate hard into the side of her head and sent her sprawling. Ben bent down to grab at her but Redwing leapt forward and kicked Ben full in the face with a hoof and he sprawled back in a spray of blood.

Lily staggered to her feet and ran out the door of the stall, Redwing at her heels. There in front of the house sat Ben and Jake's trucks, but still her Mom had not returned. She ran to the house, flung open the door, and yelled, "Ben's been kicked by the horse!" She rounded the corner of the small foyer and saw Jake struggling to rise from the couch, setting the Jack Daniels bottle on the end table. "Call the ambulance, he's hurt bad." she yelled.

Before Jake could get to her she ran back outside, where Redwing waited. "Come on, boy!" she cried, "We got to get you out of here before Jake shoots you." She led Redwing around the barn to the field and let him through the gate, shutting it again. Then she walked back to the front of the barn as Jake came stumbling out of the house.

She followed Jake into the barn where he ran to Ben, who was struggling to sit up, sputtering blood and teeth from the ruins of his face. "Fuffin' hoss!" he sputtered, "kithed me in the fathe fow no weason." He rolled over, puking up the supper Lily had made and roaring slurred and muffled obscenities.

Jake was on his cell phone with the 911 operator, cussing into the phone. "we can't wait no goddamn two fucking hours for an ambulance." He paused a moment, then said, "I'm just gonna drive him in to fucking Grand Junction myself. Thanks for fucking nothing!"

"Come on, Boy." said Jake as he bent to help Ben to his feet. "We gotta get you to the hospital." He gasped when he saw the wreck of his son's face. Bens nose was crushed sideways, his cheek was caved in, and many of his front teeth were missing. "Goddamn fucking horse messed you up bad!" he cried. "I'm gonna fuckin' kill that fucker!"

Lily darted back out the door as Jake escorted Ben to his pickup and helped him into the cab. "I'll deal with you when I get back!" yelled Jake as they drove off spitting gravel from the tires.

Lily went back into the house and then to her parent's bedroom, digging through the nightstand drawer for a few moments and withdrawing a black Ruger 38 caliber pistol and an extra magazine of ammo. She went to her room and grabbed a pink hoodie from the closet doorknob, donning it and stuffing the gun and ammo into its pockets.

Then she went back to the couch and waited for Jake to return.

Chapter 4: Gonna Be Free

She woke to the sound of the truck coming up the driveway. She sat up quickly, thumbing on the TV and turning up the sound. *Pulp Fiction* came on, Samuel L. Jackson shouting, "..and I will strike down upon thee with a great vengeance and furious anger those who attempt to poison and destroy my brothers." Bang! Bang, bang, bang.

The door slammed open and Jake stomped into the living room trailed by Ben. Ben shuffled along, his face wrapped in bandages, obviously heavily sedated and suffering. The gunfire and shouting on the TV continued.

The men went down the hall to Ben's room for a minute or two before Jake came stomping back, booming, "You little fucking bitch. Ben told me how you fucking turned that horse on him." He marched up in front of her, reaching down for her.

She glared up at him as he approached, then drew the gun and fired point blank into his ample gut. Bang! Her ears rang and he humped over wide eyed, grabbing at her. She fired again, bang, and he staggered back. Then she stood and emptied the magazine into him as he reeled and fell splattering blood. Bang, bang, bang, bang, bang.

Her ears rang and her voice sounded muffled as she yelled, "Fuck you, Jake!" Through gritted teeth she muttered in tones rising to a scream. "You will never lay hands on me again. You killed my Mom! Fucking murderer! You …"

She looked down at the dead man full of bloody holes. "Murderer!" she thought. "Murderer. Fuck I gotta get out of here before Ben gets up and calls Sherriff Sandborn. I gotta go back to Cali tonight."

She hurried to her room and dug through her clothes for her sexiest outfit, loading the rest of her favorite clothes into a duffle bag. Then she darted across the hall to the bathroom, locked the door, and stripped out of her blood spattered and sweaty clothes, throwing them into the trash can.

As she showered she felt as if she was washing away her whole grimy life since her Father had died, washing Jake and Ben away with the blood swirling down the shower drain. When she emerged dripping wet from the shower she felt exhilarated, terrified, and free.

Quickly she dried herself with a clean towel, pausing motionless for a moment with the soft towel over her face, eyes shut and trembling. When the trembling subsided, she draped the towel over the curtain rod and faced the mirror naked.

"The old Lily is gone, washed away down the drain." she thought calmly. "This is the new Lily, and no-one will ever treat me like that again."

She pulled on a pair of cutoff short shorts, a blouse she tied at the waist, and a pair of cowboy boots. She reloaded the pistol and stuffed it into her little brown leather handbag. Then she put on makeup, as she had seen her Mom do before they came to Nucla and the old family ranch.

Then she went outside to the barn and grabbed Redwing's red halter and reins. She walked to the field and called Redwing, who quickly came running up to her. "Good boy!" she said, "We're going for a ride!"

She climbed up on his back, caressing his soft neck and hugging him for a few long moments. Then she said, "Let's run!" and kicked him into a gallop. They ran up the dirt road to the rim of the canyon, flying along the twisting double-track atop the cliffs.

Never before had she felt such a thrill, so much freedom. She felt as fast and free as the wind. As she rode the moon rose huge and bright over the purple silhouette of the distant San Juan Mountains. The wan moonlight illuminated the Pinon, Juniper, and sagebrush covered cuestas and mesas between with a magical surreal light.

At the old three-wire gates, she goaded Redwing on and he leapt over the wires, bounding down the ridgeline toward Naturita at a full gallop. His eyes were wide and bright and his snorting exhalations were wisps of mist from his wide nostrils as his flanks lathered sweat. He seemed as excited and afraid as she was.

Chapter 5: Jacked

Her path took her near several other houses, and she spotted the Sherriff's white SUV with the golden star logo parked outside Sherriff Sandborn's place. At his gate, she slid off Redwing and climbed the fence gripping the post and stepping over on the wires.

Then she hurried over to the SUV and let all the air out of the tires. "At least it'll take him a little longer to get going after me when his good buddy Ben comes along telling lies about me." she thought. Back to the fence she ran, climbing over quickly and remounting Redwing to continue on toward town.

The two-track dirt road ended at the paved county road, and they trotted alongside the pavement into the canyon and across the San Miguel River bridge. She turned Redwing into the alley behind the small mercantile district along the highway and stopped at the back door of the saloon.

She wrapped the reins loosely around the hitching post and took off the hoodie with the gun, draping it across the post carefully above her duffle bag. Then she went to the corner of the building, peeking around for Ben's truck.

It wasn't there so she walked around to the front door below the weathered 'Miner's Luck Saloon' sign. "After tonight I need a drink and maybe more." she thought as she sauntered to the bar, turning every head her way in her skimpy clothes. "Who wants to buy me my first round?" she asked loudly, straddling the nearest barstool. "Are there any men left in this town?"

A grimy older man sat two stools down at the bar, and he stared at her with wide eyes. A thirty-something with brown hair and an impish grin rose from a table with two others dressed in striped button-down shirts or tee shirts and jeans. He approached slowly, sitting next to her and asking, "What you drinkin', pretty lady?"

"Jack Daniels for me, sugar." she replied.

The man said, "One for the lady, and one for me, too."

The bartender filled the shot glasses without a word, sliding them to Lily and the man. Lily picked up the glass and said, "Good times and good friends," downing the shot quickly.

"Another round for me and my friends." she said, rising and taking the man's hand to lead him back to the table where his friends sat staring.

She flirted and drank with the men for several hours, losing track of how many drinks she had. The laughter had become quite loud, and the voices quite slurred when the saloon door swung open and Ben came in, his face still swathed in bandages.

He marched straight over to Lily and said, "We'w goim fo a wide," grabbing her arm and yanking her to her feet.

Lily yelled, "Fuck off, Ben!" as she struggled to break his grasp.

Ben slapped her heavily, knocking her head back and holding her up by the arm as she twisted and fell.

In a second, the brown-haired man and his friends were on their feet. The brown-haired man swung a drunk clumsy fist at Ben and Ben had to drop Lily to fend off the attack. Then the fight was on in earnest, and she rolled away, crawling to her feet groggily and running out the saloon doors.

She saw Ben's truck in the lot and stumbled over to it, pulling out her little pocket knife. She fumbled out the blade and cut all the valve stems off of Ben's tires before folding the blade and slipping it back into her pocket.

She looked around blearily and went back to Redwing and her hoodie. She untied the reins and tossed them over the horse's head to rest upon his neck, saying, "C'mon ole' Redwing, run like fire." She slapped Redwing's ass and he ran off shaking his head. Clumsily she donned the hoodie, grabbed the duffle bag, and looked around again, darting across the empty highway to the sparsely filled parking lot of the Gamma Ray Motel.

She crept around the parking lot, trying each car door, and looking for California plates. She saw none, but found an open car door and slid into the back seat to the sound of yelling from across the street. Too tired and drunk to care, she lay back on the seat and passed out.

She woke as the driver's door opened and the owner got in. He set a briefcase on the passenger's seat and stuck the key into the ignition, cranking on the engine. Lily held her breath a moment as he put his right forearm across the passenger headrest and twisted to look behind before backing out of the parking place. Then both hands were on the wheel and he drove down to the roadside, pausing for a moment for another vehicle before accelerating out onto the highway.

When they were well underway, she sat up and pressed the gun to the side of the driver's head. The older, balding man's jaw dropped and his eyes widened as he saw her pop up through the rear-view mirror.

"You just drive." said Lily as icily as she could. The man looked a bit like her Father, and she swallowed hard before continuing more softly, "Get me to L.A. and everything will be alright."

She glanced over at the tire store as they passed, and there was Ben's big truck, tires repaired, and Ben was walking out of the office, looking right at her.

"Shit!" she exclaimed, "Step on it, Man. I can't believe my shitty luck."

The driver accelerated wide eyed, as Ben's truck shot out from the gravel lot of the tire store, spitting a shower of gravel behind him.

They raced up the canyon east of town going the wrong way for California with Ben's truck speeding along behind them. "Take a right on the next road, 141 towards Slickrock and Dove Creek." she ordered. The car screeched around the corner and up another winding canyon, quickly catching up to a flatbed semi with a wide load placard hauling a big tracked excavator.

The driver said, "I can't pass, I'm stuck behind a truck!"

Ben's truck suddenly loomed behind and began honking. Lily yelled, "Pass or he'll run us off the road!"

The driver stepped down on the accelerator and pulled up around the rig as they topped out of the canyon into the barren valley beyond with Ben's truck right on their bumper. Then Ben slammed into them with the cowcatcher on the front of his truck and they veered wildly into the front of the trailer of the rig.

The car screeched as it was spun sideways and the world twisted madly. Lily flew out the window through the breaking glass, flipping like a rag doll into the sagebrush along the highway. The car rolled and was dragged under the trailer, exploding in a fireball as the crushed gas tank was ignited by the sparking steel on the asphalt.

Chapter 6: Parched

For some time, the world turned black and silent. Then sound and light began to creep back in. First the sirens, then the sound of men shouting far away. Then silence and dark again.

Again, she heard voices. She opened her eyes, or at least the right one. Her left eye was swollen shut. The light was very dim and there were stars above. She rolled to her side, wincing at the pain. Flashing red and blue light was visible from somewhere and the spiky sagebrush bit into her flesh.

The still distant voices became clearer, Ben and the Sherriff.

Ben said, "Awe you suwre she ain't hewre."

Sherriff Sandborn said something she couldn't comprehend, and Ben replied, "Dat'th Dad'th gun, suwre as shit. Gimme that!"

"Hold on, Ben," exclaimed Sherriff Sandborn, "The gun is evidence, don't get your prints all over it!"

"Then gimme some fuckin' gwoves." said Ben, and gimme the gun."

The Sherriff said, "She wasn't in the car. No telling where she is now."

"She's hewre thomewhewre." said Ben, "Keep wooking."

Panicked, she began to crawl away from the road through the spiny sagebrush, cactus, and rabbit brush. The nearly full moon rose over the jagged ridgelines of the distant hills, but she stayed low and crawled on through the pungent aroma of the sagebrush and prickly brush.

Eventually the voices and flashing lights receded and finally disappeared, and she struggled to rise. She staggered forward, but the moonlit desert seemed to spin and twist. Her mangled legs buckled painfully and she fell again. Still she crawled on through the pain and darkness until it seemed all the world was an agony of sand and thorns and moonlight, and she could not go on.

She woke again in sickening heat and blinding light. She pulled herself up upon her elbows and looked around with her one open eye. The brush had long given way to dry grass and barren earth, and she could see ledges of rock along the edge of an arroyo a few hundred feet away.

Again, she began to crawl and claw her way towards the potential shelter amid the rock ledges, and she became aware that her skimpy blouse had been torn to shreds and her bare breasts and belly were abraded and torn by the brush and sand. Finally, she reached the ledges, found a small overhang, and rolled under it.

As she drifted away, her hand closed upon a crusted metal cylinder amid some scraps of rusted metal and crumbled, bleached bone. She rolled to her back and passed out again.

Act II: Chapter 7: El Toro

At the sound of the trumpet fanfare, Enrico followed his Master out into the arena. He trotted alongside and slightly behind Senor Guzman upon his fine black steed bedecked in bright patterned caparison and silver ornamented tack. Senor Guzman himself wore fitted black pantaloons, embroidered leather boots, and a tailored, silver-buttoned black jacket over his ruffled white linen shirt.

If only he rode as well as he dressed, thought Enrico, he might make this stupid spectacle worthwhile. Still he assumed his assigned position and watched attentively as Guzman circled the arena and saluted toward the stands above.

The herald announced Guzman in a loud and lordly voice, "Senor Guzman de Villarosa y El Toro Diablo Loco!"

Then the bull was set loose, and the first pass went as expected: Senor Guzman and his steed sidestepped the charging bull, and Guzman drove his lance into the bull's shoulder. Guzman turned to the stands and saluted his wife and daughter in their high seats, incidentally reigning his horse backward somewhat awkwardly.

The bull did not linger after the first pass and whirled quickly to charge at Guzman again. Enrico yelled and waved his arms to warn his Master, and Guzman was able to dance his steed away from the deadly horns and hooves and fling a second clumsy lance into the bull's side.

Still the move left him unprepared as the bull twisted again, spinning into Guzman's horse and goring its shoulder. The horse reared wildly, kicking at the bull and trying to flee the raging beast. Down went Guzman, flung from the saddle, and the horse fell with him as he clutched the reins desperately.

In the blink of an eye, Enrico ran out toward the bull, waving his hat in the air and shouting to turn its attention away from Senor Guzman as he fell beneath his steed. The bull turned again and charged at Enrico, lowering its horns to gore him. Enrico gripped his lance tightly a couple times, getting the balance of the weapon and the cadence of the bull just right.

As the bull neared, he sprinted forward, grabbing the bull's right horn as he leapt up with all his strength. As he cleared the beast's head he flipped and drove the lance down just behind the skull through the thick hide between the skull and first vertebrae into the spine. He rode the dying bull to the ground as it collapsed and slid many feet forward in a cloud of dust.

He looked up into the stands as the roaring of the crowd turned to cheering and found himself staring right into the deep brown eyes of Rosa Guzman, his Master's beautiful daughter. With a reddening face, he tipped his hat to her and dropped to one knee atop the dead bull. With a flourish and a blown kiss, Rosa tossed him a red rose, which he caught deftly.

Again, he blushed as he stared up at her for long moments, bringing the fragrant bloom below his nose. Suddenly the screams of Senor Guzman and his horse brought him back to the aftermath of the bullfight. He turned to his fallen Master and saw that the other three cowboys had come to Senor Guzman's aid while he knelt staring at Guzman's beloved daughter.

Chagrined, Enrico rose quickly and ran to the fallen horse, calming it and helping it to rise without further injury to Senor Guzman. The beautiful horse bore a terrible gouge upon its right shoulder, but Enrico thought it would likely heal with proper treatment.

Guzman, too, rose with the aid of two caballeros. He limped forward with their support, bowing painfully in front of his wife and daughter and the many dignified spectators. His wife threw a rose to him, but he was unable to catch it and it fell to the sands near the wall.

As Guzman turned toward the gates, he saw the rose clutched in Enrico's hand as he stood leading the wounded horse. In a flash Guzman drew his sword and slashed the rose from Enrico's hand. Enrico sprang back and the horse reared up tugging Enrico away as he struggled to bring the creature under control.

Guzman lunged forward to stab at Enrico, but the roar of the crowd turned dark and he heard his daughter scream in horror and shame. He glanced up at the shocked faces in the stands and saw the obvious shame of his wife and daughter. Then he lowered and sheathed his sword and limped from the field, shrugging off the assisting caballeros.

Enrico dutifully followed, leading the black stallion through the arena gates to the stables. Out of sight of the crowd, Senor Guzman accepted the offered help to his coach. Enrico stabled the horse and called to the grooms for boiled water and ointments. He spent several hours cleaning and treating the wound before leading the horse on the long walk back to the Guzman Estate.

He stabled and fed the horse, then walked back to the shack he shared with the other caballeros. Bone weary, he lay down quietly in his bunk and immediately fell asleep.

Chapter 8: Conscripted

Suddenly he woke as a coarse cloth sack was shoved down over his head and a heavy man sat down upon him, wrenching his arms back and wrapping them in loops of rough leather. He heaved up with his hips and legs, throwing the unseen heavy man off him briefly, but the big man gripped him tighter and sat back down on his back, knocking the wind out of him.

He struggled again and a heavy blunt object thumped into the side of his head. He fell back dazed.

"Don't worry, Boy!" said a rough deep voice, "You just joined the Queen's Navy. You're going to the New World, Boy. If you want to live, you'll come quietly."

The heavy object thumped him again and he fell away into unconsciousness.

He woke in another bunk, and the swaying made him think for a moment that perhaps he had had too much to drink. Then the memory of the previous day's events came roaring back to him with his headache.

He groaned and sat up on his elbows, looking around in the grey semi-darkness. He lay on a bunk in a row of similar bunks stacked three high along the walls. His groans brought a round of guffaws and laughter from the nearest bunks.

"New recruit, eh?" sounded a nasal voice from the bunk below. "Just don't puke in here. At least make sure you get to the bucket or top deck first."

Another voice piped up, "Conscripted is better than jailed or dead. The explorer's life. Bad food, bad water, and just enough wine to keep you from caring. Gotta bring the word o' God to the savages, that's what we're doing. And providing God's church with plenty of the savage's gold."

Enrico staggered to his feet and stumbled toward the door. "Gotta piss!" he said.

"Off the rail top decks," said the second voice, "or the piss pot, but you gotta empty it yourself before it spills."

Enrico glanced at the speaker, a battered, ragged bearded fellow with hard grey eyes.

"what's your name, boy?" asked the bearded man flatly.

"Enrico Amiduras." He replied.

"Rico, then." said the man. "I'm Orlando, and this guy," he said gesturing toward another bunk, "we call Ratface."

"The name is Ferdinand!" spat Ratface, "and don't forget it."

"We haven't forgot," countered Orlando, "Ratface just suits you better."

Rico took the bickering as an opportunity to avoid further discussion, and he slipped out the cabin door to clamber up the steep stairs to the deck. He swung the door open and stepped out into the bright sunshine on the rhythmically heaving deck.

He stepped unevenly to the railing, untying the drawstring of his breeches with one hand on the top rail. For many long moments he pissed between the rails into the churning sea below, reeling with the heaving deck and relief of his straining bladder.

He saw three other tall ships in the armada, two ahead and one behind.

Then from behind him came another voice, "You. Boy."

Rico glanced over his shoulder as he finished and quickly drew up his breeches to fumble with the drawstring.

A short, sturdy man in officer's jacket and hat stood there, and asked, "What's your name, Boy."

"Rico." He replied quickly.

"Well, Rico," the officer said, "I am Bosun Alvarez, and you are on shit duty until further notice or until some other unfortunate is conscripted below you."

Rico finished tying up, and turned to the officer fully.

"Start by emptying all the piss-pots in the quarters." The officer continued, "Then we'll see if you are of any use."

Rico kept to himself, quietly fulfilling his duties and volunteering for any other tasks as he learned the ways of the ship and its captain and crew. Four horses had also been brought aboard for the expedition, and Rico took it upon himself to care for them as best he could in the tiny corral on deck.

Soon enough Ratface was again stuck with shit duty after he shirked his other duties and was caught stealing an extra portion of wine.

Rico also met the priests for the expedition, three Benedictine Friars selected to bring the Word of God to the savages of the New World. The priests were to provide spiritual guidance to the men and the expedition's leader, a general named Grajalva, who sailed aboard the flagship.

Fray De La Cruz, who led the clerical expedition, was a powerfully built dark haired man in his early thirties with a short wiry beard, hard blue eyes, and a military bearing. He stayed near the Captain and other officers, and spent little time with the men or the other friars. He spoke little of the Word of God, instead taking much interest in the armaments and proposed landing sites in the New World.

Fray Esteban followed at De La Cruz's heels like a dog, nodding his head and saying "Yes, yes!" to De La Cruz's every word.

Fray Angelico instead spent much time with the crew, helping with scullery duties and chatting with them with a kindly smile and gentle tone. Each night he led a prayer before mess, and each morning he read aloud from the Bible and spoke passionately about the mission to turn the savages away from their demon gods to the Salvation of Christ.

Angelico also taught letters to those of the crew who cared to learn, and Enrico eagerly accepted the instruction. While the other sailors gambled and drank in the mess, Enrico sat alone in his bunk, slowly working his way through a copy of the Bible lent to him by Angelico.

Though Enrico had never before been at sea, he fell into the routine of sailing easily. His natural athleticism enabled him to excel at many of the more difficult duties, and his quiet demeanor put him in good standing with Captain Abetta and the officers.

After two months and two days at sea, the call came down from the crow's nest, "Land!"

"That'll be Espanola," said Alvarez. "We'll re-supply and take two days leave here. Don't get any ideas of desertion: it's an island, and you'd be hunted down like a beast. Pretty Taina girls here, though, if you've got the coin."

The port town of Santa Domingo lay in a harbor sheltered by barrier islands along the south shore of the big island. After months at sea, the men were excited to see any port, and the new settlement had the men shouting and hustling more than they had throughout the trip.

Rico was among the last to get to take shore leave the second day with Fra Angelico and six other sailors. He was happy to help row the longboat to shore where the port bustled with activity. Two other ships sat at anchor in the harbor, but their expedition seemed to be a big event for the place.

When the longboat was beached, he leapt out into the surf, helping to drag the boat up onto the sand. Then he stood for a moment on the strand, looking up and down the beach and at the many new structures under construction and the squalid huts and shanties spread chaotically about.

Many of the buildings were rough wooden circular structures with conical thatched roofs, but the new construction bore a strong sense of Spanish architecture, and a big church, fort, and Gubernatorial Palace dominated the town.

"It is Sunday morning, and Fray Antonio Montesinos is famously pious and well-spoken." said Fra Angelico to the men. "I would welcome your company at the church."

The sailors laughed, and Orlando said, "Thanks, Fra Angelico, but We have other business to attend to." as he glanced at the alluring shantytown along the beach. Already the New World shocked Rico: Bare breasted or naked brown skinned women beckoned from some of the shanties, while near naked men worked at nets, porting, or construction.

After a brief pause, Rico replied, "I'll join you, Fra Angelico, and be glad of your company."

Angelico nodded with a smile and began walking up the beach toward the distant church.

"Who are these Tainos?" asked Rico, "I had heard that they were free people, but they look to be slaves."

"The Tainos are native to the islands of Espanola and Cuba." replied Angelico, "and they are slaves in all but name. The encomienda allots the Taino, and all the savages of the New World to repartimientos, and the encomenderos are supposed to govern the native caciques and guide them to Christ."

Rico walked silently for a few moments, watching the Taino men working and trying not to leer at the beautiful naked Taina women and girls in the obvious brothels. "Slavery in brothels and forced labor seem to me to be poor methods for conversion." he said at last.

Angelico nodded, "Indeed, they are a poor method, but gold and beautiful women are a powerful element for corruption."

They walked in silence for several more minutes before Fra Angelico said, "You must keep any criticism between us. There are many here, even among the clergy, who would have you punished for it."

Rico nodded, grimacing as he said, "Men such as Fra De La Cruz."

"Yes," replied Angelico quietly, "Men such as Fra De La Cruz." He strode several more paces, and said, "De La Cruz was an infantry commander against the Moors, recruited by Bishop Fonseca, but not for his piety. We must be careful."

Rico nodded again, and asked no more questions as they walked the rest of the way to the church.

The church itself seemed strange to Rico. It was of obvious Spanish design, but many aspects of local architecture were still in evidence, including the strange conical thatched roof and wattle walls.

The altar itself and the golden candelabra were familiar shapes, and the fronts of the pews were occupied by Spaniards, while the near-naked Tainos gathered at the back of the church, some wearing scraps of Spanish clothing.

They sat down just as Fray Montesinos took the pulpit, an unassuming man with a rough beard and disarming smile. He led with a reading from the Bible in Latin, which baffled Rico, though he joined in crossing himself and saying "Amen."

Then Montesinos looked at the Spaniards with a gentle smile and sad eyes, and began his sermon:

Tell me, by what right do you hold these Indians in such cruel and horrible servitude?

By whose authority did you make unprovoked war on the people, living in peace and quiet on their land, and with unheard-of savagery kill and consume so great a number of them?

Why do you keep them worn out and downtrodden, without feeding them or tending their illnesses, so that they die – or rather you kill them by reason of the heavy labor you lay upon them to get gold every day?

What care do you take to have them taught to know their God and Maker, to be baptized, to hear Mass and keep their Sundays and Holy Days?

Are they not Men? Have they no souls, no reason?
Are you not required to Love them as you Love yourselves?
Do you understand this? Do you not feel it?
How can you be sunk so deep in unfeeling sleep?

At that, Montesinos looked down at each and every Spanish face in the congregation with a gentle smile. Few were able to meet his gaze, and many of those met it with a glare of resentment. Among those, Rico noted, was Fray De La Cruz, who had come in behind them, and stood at the back of the church with Fra Esteban.

Montesinos ended with another prayer in Latin, and the congregation rose and filed out down the aisle. Rico thought he saw Fra De La Cruz making his way from the church toward the Gubernatorial Manse as he came out of the doorway with its heavy carven wood doors.

He did not visit the brothels, instead using what little coin he had to purchase good food and drink from a little tavern near the beach. Fray Angelico joined him, but their conversation was limited as they enjoyed the outlandish scenery and delicious exotic food and drink.

The tavern consisted of one of the many thatched timber huts with rolled wattle walls which could be closed in foul weather. Within were an array of hand carved tables and benches, and a few others sat in the shade below, sipping out of hollow gourds.

Their naked waitress, a black-haired girl of perhaps fifteen with big eyes and dark lashes brought them fried fish served with cassava bread, garlic potatoes, and a fermented, sweet amber drink she called mabi. Each time she returned to set down the wooden trenchers and gourds, she faced the men warily and backed away bowing.

A commotion arose back up the hill toward the church, and Rico and Fray Angelico turned to look from their seats on the veranda of the tavern. Fray De La Cruz, Esteban, and a dozen armed and armored men had marched back from the Gubernatorial Manse and now stood at the front of the church in an animated argument with the church caretaker.

De La Cruz held up a document from which he read loudly enough to hear even at their distance, though they could not make out the words. Soon the great doors opened and Fray Montesino came out, looking toward Fray De La Cruz as he finished reading from the document. De La Cruz lowered the document and rolled it up as he beckoned to the soldiers and stepped aside.

The soldiers came forward up the stairs to the church doors, seizing Montesinos' hands and clapping his wrists in irons behind his back. Then De La Cruz led the group back up the hill toward the Gubernatorial Manse again, the hubbub of the crowd dying away to a sullen murmur as the popular priest was led away to prison.

All too soon, the order came to return to the ship, and he found himself shoving the longboat back into the surf. When it was free floating, he heaved himself back in and sat at the oars, stroking back to the waiting ship.

The wind had come up considerably since their landing, and he had to pull hard at the oars to overcome the waves and wind. When they reached the ships, and had hoisted the boat back into its mooring, he saw that dark clouds were building on the horizon.

Chapter 9: Shipwreck

Soon the order came to hoist the anchor and make way. With the oncoming storm at their back, the ships raced along the rising swells with full sails and they rounded the point of the island before nightfall. For a time, it seemed that they had outrun the storm as the dark horizon slid behind the hilly island.

Soon, however, the island was enveloped by the oncoming storm. As the daylight waned, flashes of lightning became visible on the horizon, tracing wild patterns through the night sky and illuminating the four ships racing through the growing swells.

The night wore on, and still they outpaced the storm, bearing west in an attempt to get out of its path. Morning dawned grey and wet as the cloudbank overtook them and they spent the day fighting to secure loose rigging or torn sailcloth amid the heaving sea.

The intense winds and waves had separated the ships, and they could only occasionally see the other three vessels through the driving rain. At last the Captain called out, "We can't outrun this one, boys! Furl the sails and prepare to turn us into the waves."

The weary crew swarmed up the rigging, Rico among them, pulling at ropes and trying to straighten the billowing sailcloth. By then they could no longer see the other ships at all, even high in the rigging as they were.

Ratface was slow to climb the rigging, and even slower with the ropes, and when a great gust of wind tore at the sail, he let go the rope. The coil whisked around the stay and whipped into Orlando's face, flipping him from the rigging to plunge down still holding the rope and crash into the lower sail where he lost his grip and fell heavily to the tilting deck.

Ratface himself stared dumbly as Rico fought to secure the flapping sail. Only after Rico had successfully belayed his rope did Ratface move to grab for the trailing line. Even so, Rico was quicker, leaning deep over the stay and pulling mightily at the flapping sailcloth to get to the flailing line. Then with Ratface's help, he managed to belay the line and secure the furled sail.

They scampered back down the rigging as fast as they could as the mast bobbed back and forth with the rise and fall of the waves. Orlando slid limply along the deck into the rail stay. The bosun rushed to him, but a sudden pitch of the deck sent him flying over the rail into the churning sea.

Rico leapt the last five feet to the deck and ran to the rail, looking down for the bosun, but he was gone amid the waves. Rico grabbed Orlando by the arm, and as Ratface joined him, they dragged Orlando to the deck hatch.

"All hands get below and prepare to turn!" shouted the Captain from the wheel. They opened the hatch and lowered Orlando's limp body to the ship's cook and galley hand below. Their crew mates rushed to the other hatch, descending the steep stairs as quickly as possible.

Suddenly the ship lurched and listed hard to port as the captain and first mate pulled at the big wheel, turning the craft ponderously atop a giant swell. Just as suddenly, the ship lurched hard to starboard and there was a blinding flash of lightning. For a split second they caught a glimpse of another ship plunging down the face of the oncoming swell toward them.

Rico had just enough time to jump down into the hold before the other vessel crashed into the bowsprit and prow with a terrible crash. He thudded into the hull just as the lantern shattered and all turned to darkness.

The timbers groaned like Leviathan rising, and the deck tilted, water rushing in from somewhere. He rolled and slid along the steep slope of the deck, crashing into stowed wooden crates and other frantic men in the near total darkness. Muttering and moaning was all around him, and someone was crying softly, while another shrieked and yet another prayed frantically.

Then the boat heaved back the other way and Rico clung tenaciously to the cargo netting. On and on and on, the ship and its men were thrown back and forth with the ever-changing tilt of the deck, and up and down with the huge swells.

After some interminable time, the chorus of terrified men subsided, but the soft prayers of Fray Angelo continued on. The water had risen within the confines of the hold, and the men were again ripped from the places they had caught hold by the might of the water sloshing back and forth with the vast waves.

Again, the men collided with objects and each other as they were cast about in the dark maelstrom, until suddenly another crash sounded even greater than the one before. The ship shuddered horribly and seamed to scream as it's timbers were rent and the hull dragged along against some hidden shoal or reef.

Then the water roared in unhindered and Rico slammed again into a deck, though he did not know up from down. He clawed madly for some purchase on the deck or beams and his fingers caught many terrible splinters before catching by chance upon the latch to the top deck. The hatch flipped open and Rico half poured through the port on the now vertical deck as the ship lay on its side foundering upon the hidden shoal.

Before he could even begin to look back to his shipmates inside, another wave crashed down upon the doomed vessel, staving in the side against the reef. The ship slid forward with the force of the wave and Rico was cast free of the dying hulk to flounder in the trough between the swells. He had just enough time as the next great breaker rolled in to dive beneath the pounding curl of water and swim toward the unseen shoreline away from the collapsing ship.

When he at last swam and rolled free of the breakers on the sandy, rocky beach it was all he could do to drag himself up the beach to the thick margin of jungle marking the edge of the strand. Then Rico passed out in exhaustion.

Chapter 10: New World

The new day dawned bright and clear over the white beach and grey, cobbly margin. The jungle rose stark and tall in shades of green and brown against the pale azure sky and sea. Mosquitoes came in swarms wherever the thick foliage hid the sun, and Rico woke sweltering and itching.

Debris was strewn up and down the beach and rocky margin, and Rico saw that other survivors had mustered around a lone longboat drawn up just beyond the reach of the little breakers on the beach.

He saw Captain Abetta, Ratface, and two friars among them, but Rico estimated that only about thirty of the eighty four souls aboard the ship had survived. Somehow three of the horses had also survived and stood tied calmly in the shade of the towering jungle.

Rico rose, pissed, and made his way along the strand to the other men past the broken cargo, flotsam, and a few half-buried corpses. The broken hulk of the ship lay upon its side a few hundred feet out from shore, broken mast and partially furled sail rocking in the gentle surf still tethered by the rigging to the wreck.

As Rico approached, Captain Abetta turned to him and said, "Glad you made it, son. Few enough of us did." He clapped Rico on the shoulder and said, "You're my First now, Rico, for whatever its worth. Take two men with you out to the wreck and see what you can salvage. Be sure to get the chest from my quarters, and any papers you find, as well as armaments, supplies, and tools from below deck." Abetta pulled his keys out of a pouch at his belt, removing one from the ring and handing it to Rico.

Abetta turned to the rest of the men and said, "The rest of you check the beach for anything useful. Ferde, Carlos, and Anton, you are on guard duty."

For the first time, Fray De La Cruz turned to Rico and said, "See to it that you recover the cannon, powder, ammunition, and arquebuses first." He waited sharp-eyed for Rico to nod in acknowledgement before continuing, "Pikes, armor, and swords are the next priority."

Captain Abetta's face clouded at the usurpation of his authority and he spoke up commandingly, "We also need food and shelter, so get what you can of the provisions and tools."

Abetta turned to De La Cruz, and said, "You are in charge of the spiritual guidance for this company, but I command this crew and you will not interfere with my commands."

De La Cruz glared at Abetta with his hard eyes, but nodded and said, "Of course, Captain. I just wish to assist your new Second in discerning the priority of salvage."

Abetta matched De La Cruz's stare for a few tense moments, but Rico did not wait for further clarification, "Ratface, Hymie, with me." he said, turning to the boat. The other two joined him and they heaved the boat out into the surf, leaping in as soon as the craft began to float free.

They rowed out toward the wreck easily, though their stomachs grumbled terribly with hunger. Soon enough the boat bumped up against the vertical deck. Rico stripped off his still damp boots and torn shirt before climbing onto the broken hull.

There was no practicable way to enter the wreck from atop the hull, so Rico looked down through the clear blue water covering most of the top deck. Sure that he would not hit an obstacle, he jumped into the sea.

He plunged down deep for a moment, opening his stinging eyes to look for a safe entry into the wreck. The port he had opened in those desperate moments below decks still hung on one twisted hinge, and he could see beams of light streaking into the hold from the broken hull. He though he caught a hint of silvery motion inside before he bobbed back to the surface.

Rico swam over to the aft end of the ship where the door to the Captain's quarters lay some ten feet below the waves. He took the thong with the key from around his neck and wrapped it several times around his wrist to be sure not to lose it. Then he dove down to the door, fumbling the key into the lock and tugging on the door.

Hymie and Ratface maneuvered the boat over to Rico as he worked, staying clear of the area just above the doorway. Poised to assist, they watched carefully as Rico swam.

At first the door did not budge, so he resurfaced to catch his breath before diving down again. Then he braced his feet against the bulkhead and heaved at the door with both hands. With a pop and groan, the jammed door opened and Rico swam back up for another breath.

He re-secured the key cord around his neck and dove down into the dark cabin. The portals in the side now opened up to the sky, and beams of sunlight streamed in in a linear pattern providing enough light for Rico to locate the desk, chest, and a trunk in the gloom. First, he grabbed the chest, tugging it along the bulkhead toward the door as he swam.

He swam hard to surface with the chest, and had to cling to the timber frame to keep his prize from dragging him back down. With a struggle, Rico pulled the chest to the surface, where Hymie and Ratface pulled it into the boat.

Rico repeated the swim two more times, retrieving the trunk and a satchel of papers and scrolls from the desk.

Then Rico swam back to the open portal to the hold.

"Come on, Ratface!" shouted Rico as he treaded water above the open port, "The water is fine." The water was indeed comfortably warm, especially compared to the sweltering heat in the direct sunlight ashore.

Ratface stood up agitatedly from the thwart upon which he had been seated, looking wild-eyed at the ship and sea. "I can't swim!" he sniveled back.

"My ass you can't swim." said Rico with a tight grin, "You got to shore somehow, unlike Orlando or the Bosun. Get in."

Ratface scowled and looked back toward Hymie who still sat at the other oars. Hymie laughed and said, "Better you than me, Ratface." Hymie's smile disappeared and he added, "Get in or I'll throw you in."

Ratface looked at Rico again, then stripped his boots and jumped off the boat to leave it rocking gently as it bumped against the greater bulk of the wreck.

Ratface dog-paddled over to Rico with an ungainly stroke, craning his neck to keep his thin goatee out of the water.

"It'll take both of us to get the casks and crates out." said Rico as he continued to tread water. "First thing we look for some coils of rope. We're gonna have to tie on to the heavy stuff and haul it up, once we get it close to the port."

Ratface nodded wide-eyed and Rico continued, "We're gonna swim down inside and get some rope. It was stowed below the fore stair, so we look there first."

Rico dove down into the port and swam toward the bow inside the dark wreck with Ratface trailing behind so close at first that Rico accidentally kicked him in the face. As their burning eyes became accustomed to the gloom, they saw that much of the light streaming in through the rent hull was blocked by the floating corpses of many of the missing men, still trapped in the shattered hold.

Rico swam quickly on, but Ratface turned toward the corpses in horror. Somehow, one of the dead men moved, his pasty arm twitching. Then he suddenly rolled over, pale bloated face and bulging white eyes staring at Ratface. Ratface screamed a squeak and stream of bubbles as a four-foot long barracuda shot out from amid the bodies, trailing part of an arm streaming dark blood.

The barracuda raced out of the port, and Ratface raced out behind it as quickly as he could.

Rico rounded the stairwell and grabbed a big coil of rope, but found himself unable to swim with the heavy load. Instead he was forced to trudge along the broken hull below, climbing over beams and bulkheads until he began to run out of air and had to retreat behind Ratface.

They surfaced and took a few deep breaths. "Stay with me, man." said Rico calmly. "Ditch me again and you'll be floating down there with the others."

Ratface nodded, scrunching up his weaselly face.

Rico dove again, and Ratface reluctantly followed. Together they hauled the rope to the port, untying the end. Ratface then swam the rope end to the longboat, handing it off to Hymie, who hauled the bulk of the coil in.

Then Rico and Ratface began to swim inside the wreck, free key pieces of cargo from the cargo netting, and drag the cargo to the port. Then they would secure the cargo to the rope and Hymie would haul it in while Rico and Ratface guided the load.

Six of the cannon were mounted on swivels in strategic locations on the deck, two of which remained above water. Hymie began work detaching the nearest cannon from the deck and railing, stopping to haul up the rope when another piece of cargo was available.

They successfully retrieved three such loads, a sealed keg of powder, the wine, and a sealed cask of hard tack. Then Rico and Ratface dove into the wreck again. Suddenly a shadow fell over the wide port through which they had swum.

Into the wreck swam a big shark, just as Rico and Ratface worked to heave a heavy chest of armaments over a broken bulkhead. In a panic, Ratface dropped the end of the load and it slammed down on the broken timbers, driving a large splinter into Ratface's leg.

The shark circled the hold once, then snatched the corpse with the missing arm, dragging it back out through the port.

Ratface spat bubbles and flailed for a moment, then began frantically swimming for the port, a wisp of blood trailing behind his wounded leg. He emerged next to the wreck, shouting to Hymie for help and swimming for the longboat.

He did not see the even larger shark as it glided under the longboat toward him. Then with a snap of the huge maw, Ratface's legs were gone and he disappeared below the surface in a roil of blood.

At Ratface's screams, Hymie sprang up from where he lay across the rail near the tied-off swivel-gun working at the fastening pins. He rushed along the side of the hull and leapt back into the longboat, grabbing the harpoon stowed within.

By the time Hymie readied the harpoon, the shark had passed below the longboat again and was just an ominous shadow disappearing into the depth beyond the reef. All that remained of Ratface was a slowly dispersing cloud of blood.

Rico surfaced outside the wreck a few moments later, scrambling into the longboat quickly with the end of the drag-rope clutched in one hand. "That was a very big shark!" he said as he rolled to his back and sat against the bench. He looked around wildly for a moment, "Ratface?"

Hymie shook his head with wide shiny eyes and gulped. "Very big shark."

Rico lay back down on the bench for a few moments, closing his eyes against the bright sunlight and breathing deeply. The quiet lapping of the waves and the gentle bump of the longboat against the ship in the bright sunshine belied the danger and horror below.

Finally, Hymie rose from his seat on the longboat bench and jumped back to the wreck. Rico opened his eyes and sat up.

He retrieved the rope end from the bottom of the boat and began hauling on it, but the chest below caught against the timbers of the wreck. After coiling the end of the rope on the bottom of the boat, Rico joined Hymie in detaching the swivel gun. Together they hauled the gun to the longboat, returning to the wreck for two more of the deck guns.

As they worked they kept watch for other sharks, and indeed they saw several at first, though none matched the monster which had eaten Ratface.

At last they had the three accessible canon aboard the longboat. Rico and Hymie sat for long moments resting after their efforts before Rico said, "I've got to go back down there."

Hymie nodded solemnly. "I can go this time." he said, "The shark will only eat me if he's hungry. Fra De La Cruz has a hunger that will never end. If we don't bring him what he wants, we're dead men."

Rico looked at Hymie for a few moments and said, "I'll go. I already know where most of the useful stuff is stowed, so I should be the one to go."

At that he got up, scanned the depths below for danger, and dove in.

They worked at the salvage until the sun sank low over the jungle, and they again began to see the sinister shapes of sharks in the murk around the wreck. Wearily they rowed back to the shore.

As they landed several of the other men rushed into the surf to help drag the longboat up on the beach. The rest of the party had not been idle while Rico's little team salvaged the wreck.

Like ants, the men gathered the gear and hauled it up the beach to a path that had been hacked from some game trail into the jungle. The path led to a small clearing where some rough lean-tos had been constructed of logs, broad leafed plants, and vines.

Captain Abetta, too made his way to the longboat, addressing Rico after the longboat was safely ashore. "What did we recover?" asked the Captain.

"Three of the deck cannon," replied Rico, "a keg of powder, and a barrel of shot. Four arquebuses with shot, six crossbows with 4 dozen bolts, four halberds, and three swords. We found four armor harness as well." Rico shouldered a cask of wine before continuing, "We also got two casks of wine and a barrel of hard tack, as well as some tools and tar."

Abetta nodded thoughtfully, then asked, "Is there anything else to salvage?"

Rico nodded, adding, "There are still more rations, though they are likely spoiled by seawater, and another broken keg of powder."

Abetta nodded and turned back toward the jungle.

Rico followed, continuing, "There is also sailcloth and more rope from the rigging, as well as metal hardware which can be reworked."

Abetta followed the laden men up the beach toward the jungle path as he spoke, "You will lead another salvage party tomorrow. Well done. Where is Ferdinand?"

Rico lowered his chin and shook his head. "A shark took him." said Rico tightly, "They are near as thick around the wreck as the mosquitoes are here. Some of the dead still float within the hull, and they draw the monsters near."

There rest of the walk was spent in silence.

When they arrived at the rough camp, the men had already opened the first casks of wine and hard tack, supplemented by a few fish, coconuts, mangos, and bananas harvested locally. Fray Angelico led a brief prayer before the portions were served, but few even listened, focused as they were on their empty bellies.

The famished men devoured their rations enthusiastically, laughing and joking as they drank their portions of wine. The grim set of their jaws and the glint of fear in their eyes belied the humor, and the camp became quiet soon after the apportioned wine was gone.

Abetta set some of the men to work through the night, sawing thick logs upon which to mount the swivel-guns. Rico and Hymie exchanged glances at the shark-like grin on Fra De La Cruz's sharp face as he watched the armaments being unloaded and prepared.

Abetta, Anton, Carlos, and Ferde were outfitted with armor, halberds, and arquebuses, while Rico, Hymie, and several others were given crossbows and bolts. Rico also received a sword as befitted an officer.

Guarded by Carlos and two of the crossbowmen, the men fell to a restless, weary sleep while the swarms of mosquitoes stung at every inch of exposed skin.

Chapter 11: Aztlan

Rico awoke to shouting and rolled to sit up quickly. At the edge of the camp stood a dozen or so brown-skinned men in outlandish garb facing Captain Abetta, Fray De La Cruz, Fray Angelico, and the guards.

The three leaders wore elaborate headdresses of feathers and torques of gold over leopard skin capelets, thick ornamented belts with dagged leather skirts and sandals. Jade and gold earrings adorned their ears and noses and they spoke a vowel-rich guttural language none of the Spaniards had ever heard the like of.

The leaders were flanked by less ornamented men with spears, feathered and furred shields, and obsidian bladed weapons like a flattened mace. Rico glimpsed other near naked men armed with spears, bows and arrows, atlatl, or hollow tubes arrayed at strategic positions around the camp in the jungle.

Despite the language barrier, the two groups spoke back and forth, using wide gestures and much pointing and repetition to get their points across. After several heated minutes, the tribal emissaries beckoned to the men behind them, and baskets of fruits, dried meats, and fish were brought forward and presented to Captain Abetta and the others by men dressed only in simple loin cloths.

At that, the tension broke, and the tribesmen were invited into the camp to share the gifts of food. The wine was likewise shared, though portions were carefully controlled. Awkward negotiations continued throughout the morning, and after the food, the natives lit long wood and onyx pipes filled with strong aromatic herbs. The pipes were passed about the groups with many smiles, though the eyes of the leaders of both groups remained hard and bright.

In the end, the Spaniards understood the meeting to be an invitation to the City-State of Tetzapotitlan, where the King awaited. The Spaniards were urged to set forth immediately with the emissaries as guides, but Abetta and De La Cruz were adamant that preparations were required, and that the Spaniards would not set forth until the next day.

As soon as the feast was over, Abetta called Rico to him. Quietly Abetta told Rico, "Take a team back out to the wreck to complete the salvage operations. Be sure to get the satchel of papers from the desk in my cabin."

Rico looked at the Captain sharply for just a moment before replying, "I got the satchel from the desk yesterday." He looked around the camp briefly, adding, "It is here somewhere."

Abetta's expression darkened, and he glanced around the camp, staring hard at Fra De La Cruz for a moment. "I see." he said, "any idea who unloaded it from the boat?"

Rico shook his head, "No, Sir, I was a bit weary and distracted at the time." Rico's gaze settled for a moment on Fra De La Cruz, too, and he added, "There are few among us who can even read."

"True enough." replied the Captain. "Let's keep this a secret for the moment. Get to it."

Indeed, the party did not leave the next day, either, and the men were kept busy with salvage and the construction of tents, bags, litters, spears, and crossbow bolts from the sailcloth, rope, and salvaged metal and wood.

When at last everything was packed and the march to Tetzapotitlan began, the natives were astounded to see Captain Abetta mount one of the horses. Fra De La Cruz insisted upon riding a horse as well, claiming that it be-fitted his station as the religious leader of the group, and that the natives must see that such leadership was held great value among the Spanish if they were to be expected to convert.

The remaining horse was equipped with rude harness to drag litters bearing gear and the log-mounted cannon.

The native leaders ostensibly lead the march, followed and flanked by their warriors, but Rico noticed that some of the archers and spearmen stayed well ahead of the column, no doubt scouting. The Spanish followed close behind the natives, flanked by the halberdiers and arquebus men. Rico followed close behind these, with the column of laden crewmen behind.

They marched north along the white beaches when possible, and followed well-used trails when the beach disappeared below sea cliffs, promontories, or swamps. Each night at camp, the groups exchanged stories and gradually began to understand bits of each other's speech.

They learned that Tetzapotitlan was a vassal city-state to the vast Aztec Empire whose capitol lay far to the south and many miles inland beyond a range of mountains. Tetzapotitlan itself lay several days march to the north, and was the northernmost of the Aztec city-states, having been conquered by the southward migrating Aztecs many generations before.

They first glimpsed the city from a promontory cliff several hundred feet above the pounding surf. Several miles beyond their viewpoint to the north lay a brightly painted step pyramid with a temple atop it surrounded by a courtyard and many other adobe buildings. Thick jungle prevented sight of any of the inhabitants, but the garish colored strange architecture was impressive even from the distance.

The road had improved greatly from the rough trails they had begun their trek upon to a stone paved track large enough for a wagon. Still Rico had seen no wagon tracks or the tracks of any beast of burden. The animal tracks he did see, deer, coyote, and myriad small mammals, as well as that of some great cat did not remain on the road for long, crossing it or veering into the jungle.

As they approached the city, throngs of naked people gathered along the road, watching the procession ardently and following along as they passed. Often the people reached out to the newcomers, touching their hands, clothing and armor with awe. At last they reached a pair of great gates set into the arch of a brightly painted adobe wall. Spear wielding guards opened the gates for them, and the naked people formed a gauntlet through which they passed. A great incomprehensible cheer rose up from the natives as the visitors entered the city.

They were led through the courtyard in front of the temple to a large open tent wherein had been set a great feast. Roast boar and fowl, with an assortment of greens, colorful flatbread, and fruit were brought to them as they sat upon bright cotton blankets by beautiful naked women and girls.

Again, the wine was brought out by the Spaniards, and while the men were only allotted their usual portion, the officers were allowed more, and the native leaders were encouraged to imbibe by the Captain and Fray De La Cruz. Soon all were laughing like old friends, and some groped the naked serving girls at will.

Abetta, De La Cruz, and Angelico asked many questions, and were willing to spend the time and effort needed to convey the questions and comprehend the answers despite the language barrier, and these efforts were a source of the amusement for both sides.

One particular story seemed to be both a source of pride for the Tetzapotitlan and a source of great interest for the Spaniards, especially Fra De La Cruz. An aged sage named Cuauhcoatl came before the group and told of his ancestral homeland far to the north.

The son of the King told us a story of his ancestral homeland far to the north and the great cities of gold. The loveliest lands with seven great cities with caves and great eagles on the flanks of a mountain.

"Oh ancient Father," said Montecuhzoma, "I desire to know the true story, the knowledge that is hidden in your books about the seven caves from which our ancestors came forth, our Fathers and Grandfathers. I wish to know about the place wherein dwelt our God Huitzilopochtli, and out of which he led our forefathers.

Tlacaelel replied, "You must know, oh Great Lord, that what you have determined to do is not for strong or valiant men, nor does it depend upon skill in the use of arms in warfare. Your envoys will not go as conquerors, but as explorers. They will seek out the place where our ancestors lived. They will try to find the place where our God Huizilopochtli was born.

As the feast closed, each of the men was led to his quarters in the nearest of the adobe buildings by one of the beautiful serving girls. The two-story structure had numerous rooms equipped with comfortable cots and cotton blankets.

The officers were given individual rooms, while the men were assigned to four shared rooms. The women made it plain that they had been given to the men for their pleasure, and few of the men had ever experienced a better night.

Chapter 12: Blood and Gold

The next morning dawned bright and warm, and the priests summoned them to the courtyard, where a great throng had assembled before the step pyramid temple. To great fanfare, the most beautiful girl Rico had ever seen was led through the courtyard and up the steps of the pyramid by two plumed and gold bedecked priests.

As the procession reached the altar at the top of the pyramid, there was a flash of fire within the little stone temple, and a garishly adorned priest appeared through the smoke. He wore an even more ornate headdress of feathers, a leopard skin cape, gold belt, torque, bracelets, rings, and nose ring. He held aloft a feathered black obsidian dagger in one hand and a mirror of polished obsidian in the other.

The girl was ceremoniously stripped of the feathered headdress and golden jewelry which had been her only clothing by the two priests who had led her to the altar. Then she lay down upon the altar with a serene smile and heavy-lidded dull eyes.

The priest stepped up to the altar, handed the mirror to the priest to his left, and raised the dagger with a flourish. Then as the other priest held the mirror before the girl's beautiful face, the high priest drove the obsidian blade down between her beasts.

Blood sprayed out like a fountain, and the priest drew the blade downward as he chanted incomprehensibly. Then he handed the dagger to the third priest and reached down to the poor girl upon the altar with both hands. Gripping both sides of her breastbone, he spread her ribs, reached in, and tore out her heart, holding it aloft as it spurted her hot lifeblood all over himself and the altar.

A roaring cheer arose from the crowd, and cries of horror from the Spanish. Rico's face grew ashen, and he turned to look at Captain Abetta. Abetta, pale as Rico, ground his teeth and turned his heel on the spectacle, marching toward the quarters as he said, "Men! To me."

Rico hurried after Abetta, glancing around at his fellows. To a man they shared the expression of utter horror, but for a moment Fra De La Cruz smiled his shark's smile at the spectacle before he turned to join the others.

They marched into the building, and Captain Abetta said, "Arm yourselves, and see to the cannon. We are leaving Tetzapotitlan and these demon worshippers, and we will fight our way out if need be."

Fra De La Cruz strode into the room, saying, "We must destroy this temple in the name of God, if we are to hold ourselves as true Christians!" He looked around at the men, bright eyed and impassioned. "God will grant us victory if we strike now with great certitude of purpose!"

He looked now at Captain Abetta, who swallowed and nodded, "Make ready, this abomination cannot stand."

To Rico it seemed that De La Cruz's ardor turned then from victory to avarice as he contemplated the spoils.

Rico donned his breastplate, cuises, vambraces, and morion, and strapped on his swordbelt before fetching a quiver of crossbow bolts. Then he helped to load and arm the cannons, checking each as it sat mounted to its log.

Abetta said, "Rico, Carlos, and I will take the horses. When we are mounted and ready, I will call the attack. Cannon crew, you will take out the temple and the gates first. The rest of us will charge the priests. If we can kill them quickly, the natives may rout. If not, it will be a hard fight to get out of this."

Rico said, "Hymie, Guillome, and Martin, arm yourselves, then saddle and prepare the horses."

Captain Abetta, Rico and Carlos emerged from the building a few minutes later, trying to meet the smiles of the natives as they mounted the waiting steeds. Then they turned their horses toward the temple, still thronged with near naked savages and the demonic priests, who they saw with renewed horror had flayed the beautiful maiden, and the head priest now wore her skin as a cape.

At that sight Abetta screamed "For God and all that is good, attack!"

Then Rico found himself spurring hard to keep pace with Abetta and Carlos as they drove their warhorses into the crowd. Boom, boom, sounded the arquebuses, then all was a chaos of blood and noise.

Rico fired his crossbow ahead, but did not even see where it hit, and he dropped it as his horse crashed into the mass of naked humanity. Men and women fell before the horsemen screaming with fear as they tried to run. He drew his sword and slashed down at an upturned face as it screamed up at him before it parted in a splash of blood.

Rico found himself screaming, too with the rage and horror and fear. The horses surged through the crowd, pressing toward the temple pyramid, then the cannon roared behind him, and the little temple atop the pyramid splintered into shards of sharp stone, throwing one of the priests to tumble down the steep steps and crunch upon the stone terrace.

Then Rico neared the stairs, and the native guardsmen rushed at him with spears. With another scream, a spear tore into his horse's chest as the horse crushed the spearman. Rico leapt for the other spearman, catching the spear beneath his boot as he chopped into the man's neck and shoulder and landed with his knee on the man's cracking sternum.

He tore the sword free of the carnage and sprinted up the steps toward the priest in the bloody skin cape. At the top of the stair, the priest dodged behind the altar and the flayed corpse. Rico lunged with the sword, but the priest deflected the thrust with the dagger and shouted something at Rico. Rico roared back at the priest, jumping forward to slash at him.

The third priest jumped forward with a spear, but Rico simply chopped it in half as he drove forward and thrust his sword. The priest fell back, the sword in his guts sliding free, and then Rico was slashing again.

This time the sword shattered the shiny obsidian dagger, carving deep into the arm holding it. The high priest screamed again as Rico sheared his head neatly from his shoulders, and it seemed to scream on as it bounced and rolled down the steep stairway to land at Captain Abetta's feet.

Rico watched from the top of the stairs as the crowd fled screaming in every direction. Abetta reached down and picked up the high priest's head by the headdress, holding it aloft before driving it down onto the spike at the end of Carlos' halberd.

To Rico atop the pyramid it looked as though the path of the Spaniards was paved with blood and corpses.

"Take what you can!" shouted Abetta, "but do not stray far. The enemy may regroup. Keep whatever women you choose, but do not dally. We leave soon."

Fra De La Cruz spoke up commandingly, "It is given to us by God to rule over these savages! They are fit only to serve us in the name of God. Kill any who will not obey, and take the others as enocomiendo."

The Captain continued on, "Carlos, Anton, Ferde, set up a perimeter with watch on the building tops. The rest of you, pillage but stay close. Fray Angelico, please count the men and see to any injuries." He turned to Rico, "Rico, with me."

Abetta stormed up the steep steps of the pyramid to Rico, huffing from the exertion of the battle and climb. When he reached the top, they spent long moments gazing out over the city. The pyramid upon which they stood occupied the center of a great walled plaza with flat topped two-story adobe apartment dwellings at each corner.

The great dining canopy and many other lesser tents and huts were arrayed about the courtyard, and the men could be seen raiding these for food and supplies. A great many other lesser buildings and huts could be seen where the jungle was thinned beyond the walls.

At last Abetta said, "We cannot hold this plaza against so many for long, especially if we start taking slaves and slaughtering villages."

Rico nodded, still mute from the recent horror still on display before his eyes. He tried not to see the flayed body on the altar and the heaps of dead at the foot of the pyramid, instead pondering the strategic points of the view.

"They will amass and return to attack us soon." agreed Rico after a few moments. "Their fear and shock will wear off when they regroup."

Fray De La Cruz finished talking to Anton and Ferde, then began to ascend the steps toward Abetta and Rico. "He is near as ungodly as they are," said Abetta, "and even more dangerous."

Rico nodded agreement, and added, "He will foment a mutiny and become a tyrant, if he can."

Abetta answered with a nod, "We must be very careful."

When De La Cruz reached the top, he smiled his shark's smile again and said, "I believe there are stairs within the temple leading deeper into the pyramid. That is likely where we will find much of the gold and treasure."

As Rico and Abetta turned to look within, De La Cruz said, "After you, gentlemen."

Abetta nodded at Rico and Rico entered the dark, broken temple, looking about. Indeed, a stone table within held many artifacts of gold, jade, and obsidian. A thick, woven rug covered the floor beyond the table, and Rico slid it aside with a foot to reveal a wooden trap door beneath.

De La Cruz knelt beside the headless body of the high priest for a moment, picking up the obsidian mirror and stripping the gold torque, belt, and rings from the body. These he placed carefully into one of the sailcloth sacks from the wreckage. Rico was struck by the reverence De La Cruz showed kneeling before the dead man and his gold, and he knew what Fra De La Cruz truly worshipped.

Then Rico drew his sword again, sidestepping down the narrow steep stairwell. At the bottom of the stair lay a tiny landing and another richly painted door. Rico pulled the latch and shoved open the door, jumping back as the torchlight briefly illuminated a snarling leopard perched upon a stone table within.

The door swung closed again, but all was quiet in the narrow corridor and the room beyond. Rico handed the torch to Abetta, who was close behind him. Then he gripped his sword pommel a few times and pushed open the door again.

There was the snarling leopard, just as before, with sparkling green eyes and bright coat shining in the torchlight. Still the leopard did not move, and Rico saw that it was not a living creature. He pushed the rest of the way into the small room, sword at the ready, but there was no immediate danger.

Instead he saw an altar loaded with treasure, not the least of which was the leopard itself. Its eyes were jade and ruby, and it was enameled superbly in gold and black. At its crouching paws atop the table and stacked against the walls was a vast array of gold and jade figurines and jewelry, as well as ornamental staves and daggers of obsidian and jade set in gold and wood with a great many brightly colored feathers and furs.

The three men stood slack-jawed in awe for many long moments before any of them moved. Finally, De La Cruz spoke up in a hushed voice with glinting eyes of gold and red, "With this treasure in our coffers I will be the first Bishop of the New World, and you shall be Governor."

Rico stared at De La Cruz blankly for a few seconds, and feared that his revulsion for De La Cruz showed plainly in his face. De La Cruz, however, and Abetta as well, still gaped at the vast treasure, and their grand visions of power and wealth showed plainly upon their ruddy torchlit features.

"We cannot tell the men the true extent of this treasure." said Abetta at length, "or we must fear each moment for mutiny and larceny."

De La Cruz nodded eagerly. "Our secret, yes." replied De La Cruz quietly.

Rico too nodded, "Yes, our secret." He paused and said, "It will be difficult to transport."

"Yes," said De La Cruz, "and it will be confiscated by Governor Ovando if word of this gets to Espanola."

"With the loss of the ship," said Abetta, "we will have to find a safe place to settle, at least until we can build another ship capable of the trip to Espanola."

"We should go north," said De La Cruz, "and find the Seven Cities of Gold."

"We do not have the men or arms to conquer and hold even one city." said Abetta.

"We need only report upon the location of the cities," replied De La Cruz, "and provide some samples of our great treasures directly to Bishop Fonseca or Queen Isabella. They will eagerly fund a greater, better armed expedition with us at its head."

"North, then," said Abetta, nodding, "to find the seven cities of gold."

"Explorers, not conquerors," said Rico, "as the sage said it would be."

De La Cruz glared at Rico briefly with his firelit eyes shining, but he said nothing.

"Have litters made for the horses," said Abetta, "they will have a very great and valuable burden."

Rico was sent to fetch more containers for the treasure as De La Cruz and Abetta packed what they could in the sailcloth sacks and inventoried the rest. Rico returned twice with wooden chests, which were also filled and loaded.

The leopard proved to be lacquered wood, and was left broken on the floor beside the table when the three men at last dragged and carried the heavy chests and sacks up the steep steps of the shaft and down the equally steep pyramid steps.

The litters were loaded with plundered food and treasure, and the men had their way with the captive women before night fell. Despite their sated weariness, none of the men slept well that night for fear of sudden attack.

No attack came that night, and at dawn they harnessed the litters to the horses and attached two long handles to each log-mounted cannon. They set forth led by Abetta, De La Cruz, Rico, and Carlos. The men and the cannon came next, with a string of 38 women roped together by their necks trailing the cannon and followed by the horses and a rearguard of six crossbowmen. Anton and Hymie were sent ahead to scout.

The ambush came without warning: suddenly the air buzzed with darts from the weak native bows and a chorus of whooping sounded as masses of near naked spearmen burst from the foliage ahead and to both side of the column.

An arrow glanced from Rico's helmet and another bounced off his breastplate before the first of the savages got to him. He raised his crossbow and loosed a bolt which drove into the gut of the first spearmen.

As he fell screaming, a second lunged in with his spear. Rico turned as the spear tip broke upon his breastplate, slashing off the spearman's left forearm. The nearest cannon roared and the mass of enemies bearing down upon the head of the column splattered into the jungle.

The charge broken, the screams of the savages turned to cries of fear and they turned and fled back into the jungle, many more falling to a blast of the second cannon.

Rico looked around at the column. A slim arrow protruded from Carlos' thigh above his cuises, and Captain Abetta bled from a deep cut to the face, but the rest of the Spaniards he could see were uninjured.

He hurried back along the line to assess the condition of the group. One of the captive women was down moaning in pain and struggling with an arrow in her side, and the two nearest women in the string had to kneel next to her to avoid strangulation by the tether. The women tried to comfort their injured companion, but she was beyond hearing them.

Farther back one of the crossbowmen, Guillome, was also down with another of the slim arrows imbedded in his lower back. He lay glassy-eyed upon the ground, groaning softly.

"Report, Rico!" shouted Captain Abetta.

Rico hurried back to the head of the column, saying, "Guillome and one of the women are down with arrows in the guts, but everyone else is pretty much intact."

"Get them on the litters," said Abetta to Rico, "we keep moving." He turned toward the back of the column, shouting, "On your feet, men. Get the wounded on litters. Move out!"

The men hurried to comply, and Fra Angelico moved to the wounded, helping them to the litters and staying with them as the column got underway again. Fra De La Cruz watched as they were carried to the litters, and he shook his head, turning to Captain Abetta.

"Those two will not long survive those injuries." He said. "Far better we grant them a merciful death now, lest we endanger the whole party."

Captain Abetta said, "We will at least give God some time to do some healing before we grant your kind of 'mercy'."

"Before I received the call to serve God as a member of the clergy, I was a Commander against the Moors." said De La Cruz with his shark's smile. "We cannot afford such sentimentality at times like these. We must fortify ourselves against such weakness and do what must be done."

"I have heard about your career in the military," said Abetta, "and it was no calling from God that caused you to resign your office. I remind you again that I am in command of this expedition, and we will not be engaging in the type of cruelty which got you expelled from the military. We will make every attempt to heal them before any of your 'mercy' is administered."

De La Cruz glared at Abetta openly, and Rico could see that Carlos, too, was listening to the exchange with interest. "I have the ear of Bishop Fonseca, and he will hear every detail of your irresponsibility in this and other matters."

Abetta bristled, "Bishop Fonseca is a world away, and it will require cooperation and considerable luck for you to ever get him your little report. Remember your place here or you may be the first to taste your own brand of 'mercy'"

At that, Carlos turned toward Abetta, half lowering his arquebus at the Captain, while Rico laid his hand on his sword pommel and stepped between them.

Undaunted, Captain Abetta marched on, and after a moment, the others followed. They found Anton and Hymie laying sprawled on the trail. Anton's body had been stripped of armor and weapons and he lay in a pool of blood with his face and body torn and pierced many times by spears and obsidian bladed clubs.

Hymie, too, lay in a heap with a pool of blood about his head. As Fra Angelico examined him, he groaned and rolled to his back trying to sit up. Blood still streamed weakly from his torn scalp, but his skull was intact. Angelico and the slave girl the Tetzapotitlani had given him, Mahari, carefully bound and treated his wounds.

He also suffered from an arrow wound to the back, but the slender arrow had glanced off his shoulder blade and did not inflict serious damage. After treatment, he insisted upon walking with Mahari and Angelico for the rest of the day's march.

At the first rest, Carlos casually walked up to the litters, picking up the injured woman and laying her beside the path as he slit her throat. Guillome was already dead.

Carlos had begun limping after the arrow was removed from his thigh, and he would not allow Fra Angelico to examine or treat the wound. His limp had become quite pronounced, and he was red-faced and sweating with every march. In the evening he was quiet and pale, and at the second camp, Captain Abetta insisted that Fra Angelico be allowed to treat the wound.

The arrow puncture site had swollen and reddened, oozing pus when pressure was applied. Angelico asked for a portion of wine to be boiled, which he applied to the wound after careful washing with the hot water. To his credit, Carlos remained stoically silent throughout the treatment.

As Angelico began to wrap the wound in sailcloth bandages, Mahari put her hand on his arm, saying something in her language which only Angelico seemed to understand. She then looked around the campsite at the surrounding foliage, selecting a low plant with sharp pointed fuzzy leaves.

She plucked some of these, shoved them into her mouth and chewed vigorously for a few minutes. Then she spat them back out into her hand, returned to Angelico and Carlos, and applied the wad of masticated plant materiel to the arrow wound.

She then spoke again in her language, indicating with gestures that the bandages should be applied over the balm.

Each of the captive women had been given by the Tetzapotitlan leaders to one of the Spaniards, and most of the men had taken the women as consorts or slaves. Fray Angelico, however, treated Mahari more as an apprentice, teaching her Spanish as they marched and learning as much of her language as he could.

Enrico listened in whenever he could, and took Angelico's relationship with his encomienda as an example. He still took sexual pleasure with his woman when the opportunity for privacy arose, but he asked her many questions and never treated her harshly. He learned that her name was Nahana, and that she had been taken captive from a tribe the Tetzapotitlani called the Chichimec, or Naked People.

The Naked People lived to the north of Tetzapotitlan, and spoke yet another unfamiliar language, though Nahana spoke primarily Nahuatl, the language of the Aztecs and their vassal states.

The Tetzapotitlani did not pursue the party as they fled north, and over the weeks, the thick jungle receded, replaced by palms along the beach and scrubby thorny brush farther inland. The air was drier, and the mosquito swarms declined, replaced by biting black flies.

They saw few people, and those from a distance before they turned and fled at the sight of the intruders. Once they saw a number of canoes some distance out at sea, but these, too, fled on sight.

Soon after, they came upon a small fishing village at the mouth of an inlet. Even before the group sighted the village, they heard cries of alarm from ahead, and they found the village abandoned. They looted whatever food they found, which included some coconuts and mangoes, as well as a mess of fresh fish in a basket.

"Is this your village?" asked Rico of Nahana while the men were searching the village for plunder.

Nahana nodded solemnly before answering in Spanish, "Si, Senor Enrico."

Rico smiled, and said, "We will not be raiding for prisoners, and we do not sacrifice people to God, as the Aztecs do for their demon gods."

Nahana nodded again, swallowing before saying with a sad smile, "You are kind, Senor Rico, as is Fra Angelico." She paused as if searching for words, then continued, "Fra De La Cruz and Senor Carlos are cruel, and would make better Aztecs than Christians."

Rico nodded with a frown, saying, "You are very wise, Nahana, but you must keep your feelings towards De La Cruz and Carlos a secret. They would harm you if they knew."

"This I know, Senor Enrico." she said. "I hope that they do not find any of my people here."

Enrico nodded again with a gentle smile, "That is my hope as well, beautiful Nahana."

Nahana blushed and smiled widely. Their quiet moment together was short-lived as the sounds of rape cut through the warm air, stripping away the smiles and leaving Nahana and Enrico to hang their heads in sadness and shame.

The screams and rough laughter continued for many long minutes, and Rico recognized the male voice as that of Carlos. Rico rose and stomped off in the direction of the sounds, but a sudden piercing shriek ended the screams.

Immediately afterward, Hymie shouted from somewhere ahead, "You had no right to kill her! You are a villain!"

"I have every right to fuck or slaughter these heathens as I see fit!" roared Carlos. "Get out of my sight or I'll kill you, too."

Rico broke into a run, Nahana following and shouting to him in her native language. Rico raced between the huts, glancing into the semi-darkness of the interiors as he neared the argument. At the doorway of a hut he saw Hymie standing with a sprung crossbow in his hands.

Hymie turned to Rico with a frown, saying quietly, "He was aiming to shoot me with the arquebus."

Rico slowed, nodding as he looked into the hut to see Carlos splayed naked across the bloody body of a young brown skinned woman or girl. The crossbow bolt protruded squarely from the center of his chest, and the arquebus lay on the dirt floor near at hand.

"Run," said Rico quietly, "run as fast as you can into the jungle and pray that Nahana's people are kinder than Fra De La Cruz."

Up behind Rico came Nahana and Fray Angelico, and Rico heard De La Cruz say, "Yes, run, so that we can shoot you down like the heathens you so love."

Rico whirled to face Fray De La Cruz, "It was self-defense, Carlos would have shot him, and these were not Aztec demon-worshippers."

Captain Abetta, too ran up to the group gathered in front of the hut just as De La Cruz said, "He has murdered an officer in the Queen's Military, and he will hang for it."

Abetta glared at De La Cruz and the others, gritting his teeth as he roared, "I am in command of this expedition! You will not undercut my authority on this matter or any other! I did not authorize any killing of unarmed women, nor does the Bible sanction such wanton slaughter. Hymie was enforcing my will in this matter, and if Carlos elected to attack him for it, he received justice on the spot."

De La Cruz glared back at Abetta for a moment before he smiled his shark's smile again, "Are you denying the encomienda provided by Bishop Fonseca and Queen Isabella herself granting us dominion over the savages?"

"The encomienda is to guide the savages and lead them to Christ, not no excuse wholesale rape and murder!" shouted Abetta. "Enough off this! We march in fifteen minutes. All hands assemble for march!"

As the argument raged, the men had gathered around, assembling naturally into factions behind the Captain and Fray De La Cruz, and they were slow to return to their tasks. Many were the hard glances at both the Captain and De La Cruz.

While the Spaniards were distracted, all the captives except Nahana and Mahari ran off into the jungle. Several of the men demanded that the party pursue the escaped women, but both Captain Abetta and Fray De La Cruz agreed that they should instead march on unburdened by the captives. The men grumbled but continued preparing for the march.

The march did resume shortly, and the party was quiet for the rest of the day, and that night's camp as well. Nahana willingly joined Rico in his bedroll and he fell asleep feeling like the luckiest man in all the New World.

For seven days more they continued north along the seashore, turning inland to avoid swamps and impassable terrain as needed. They encountered other small villages, always empty at their approach, though they were often able to plunder food from the settlements. Increasingly, Nahana and Mahari were the subject of lustful glances from the men, and whispers whenever they or Enrico were out of earshot.

Fra Angelico continued to hold prayers each morning, meal, and nightfall. After a week of this, Fra De La Cruz stood as Angelico began, saying, "We have all heard this pacifist's perspective on the Encomienda proclaimed by Bishop Fonseca in the name of God."

Angelico turned to face De La Cruz, his customary smile fading as he bowed his head slightly in deference.

'The Encomienda is not just a call for us to lead them gently as lambs," said De La Cruz, "but also that we take them as lions to serve our needs as we establish God's church here in these heathen lands. Here, far from the comfort of good Christian women, it is given to us as Christian men to take what we will of the heathen, and to guide and take to wife those of them as will listen."

De La Cruz looked around sharply at each face in the group, shark's smile and hard bright eyes piercing as he said, "We cannot continue to allow the heathen to slink away from their hovels to avoid us as we enact the will of God. We are commanded to take these savages into our Encomienda if possible, and to command or dispatch them as we see fit."

Nahana and Mahari exchanged worried glances and Rico's jaw clenched as he struggled to remain stoic. De La Cruz continued, "Let us thank God for the bounty he has provided for us in this struggle against the heathen. God grant that we may use his provision to give us the strength of body and will to claim these lands and peoples for His glory. Amen."

As had become customary at supper, Rico, Nahana, Mahari, and Fra Angelico joined Captain Abetta as they sat on a colorful cotton blanket taken from their quarters in Tetzapotitlan.

This time they ate silently for some time before Fra Angelico spoke after looking around to assure that no others were in earshot. "We must act to protect the women before De La Cruz and his cohorts use the Encomiendo to make them whores for the whole company." He looked in turn at Mahari and Nahana with a gentle smile before turning to Abetta and Rico. "You must marry the women before God if you wish to protect them, else I fear they will again be roped by the neck and led like beasts to be bred by the worst of this company."

Rico smiled at Nahana, taking her hand in his. She smiled weakly back at him as Angelico looked on. Mahari, in turn looked first at Fra Angelico worriedly, then stoically to the Captain. Captain Abetta looked down for a few long moments before saying, "I have a wife and family back in Spain. I cannot marry Mahari, though I would not see her turned to slavery."

"I can speak to another of the men, perhaps Hymie," said Angelico, "but it will not carry the same gravitas with the men." He paused a moment, then continued, "It may grant us time, however."

Hymie proved to be thrilled to exuberance at the prospect of marriage to Mahari. His boyish grin and the joyful way he seized and kissed Mahari's hand at the suggestion of marriage brought warm smiles to the faces of the other marriage conspirators. Even Mahari's flat expression expanded into happy laughter.

They scarcely noticed the resentful hatred in the glares of the worst of the other men, nor the shark's grin of Fra De La Cruz as he did notice.

The weddings were held the next morning at dawn as the sun rose red above the sea. The women wore simple white cotton dresses and woven circlets of flowers and feathers as they faced the men and struggled with the Spanish vows.

Hymie's grin and enthusiasm proved contagious, and the whole party laughed and smiled with him or at him as he looked at Mahari with the adoration of a puppy. He fumbled and stammered his own vows as much as the women, but no one could doubt his sincerity.

All too soon, the march was on again, and the smiles were gone soon after the sunrise.

The weeks wore on, the heat and endless toil wearing away at them as the plodded on and on. Grumbling had turned to angry outbursts and the whispers of jealousy and lust became a continuous chorus whenever the women were out of sight of the officers. Hymie had taken to scouting with Federico since Anton's death.

Most of the men had grown thick beards as shaving and trimming them became more difficult, but Hymie's beard remained sparse and short, and the men had taken to calling him "Taino Boy." They joked and talked of the women as witches who had turned the Captain, Fray Angelico, Rico, and Hymie into heathens.

At length, they came upon the mouth of a mighty river, which they could not ford or consider swimming. They turned inland along the banks, ascending into hilly country as they drew further and further from the sea.

At the top of a ridgeline, they saw a golden city of blocky multi-story buildings below in the light of the setting sun. Their eyes glinted with excitement, and there were many whispers of "Cibola, the City of Gold!" The excitement was short lived, for as they approached and the golden sunset faded, they realized that the structures were just adobe and wood.

The people there had not yet heard of the Spanish invaders, and they rushed from their little villages to hoot at the strangers and paw at them with gentle hands as they passed. Food and shelter were given to them at each village, and Captain Abetta made it clear that he would not tolerate any raping or pillaging.

With the help of Mahari and Nahana, and increasingly Fra Angelico and Enrico, they were able to ask about the origins of the Aztec migration south, and the probable whereabouts of the Cities of Gold, called Cibola.

On and on they followed the river ever higher as the hills and valleys grew to mountains and deep valleys and canyons. At times, they had to leave the river far below them as they struggled through the steep terrain. The villages became more scarce, and the people less trusting, and the men took to sending out hunting parties to feed the group. The plants were no longer familiar to Nahana and Mahari, and the group began to grow lean and hungry.

Chapter 13: Gods or Demons

Twenty-two more days marching brought them to a great wide valley surrounded by mighty peaks on all sides. The valley was dotted with little villages surrounded by fields of maize fed by a network of ditches and canals. They were met by a party of armed warriors in leather and bone armor with painted stripes and patterns on both their faces and clothing and headdresses of leather and feathers.

Though they bore bows and arrows and spears, they approached slowly in plain sight of the strangers and they did not brandish their weapons in a threatening way.

The leader approached alone, holding up an open palm to show no violent intent. Captain Abetta approached with wary confidence and they spoke back and forth in an attempt to find common language, though Rico and the others could not hear the words. Soon the speech added a great many gestures, and the Captain understood that the natives were offering them hospitality.

The natives spoke a language unknown to them, but Mahari found that they understood a few words of Nahuatl, and they bristled when they heard it. Mahari calmed them somewhat by telling them that the party was not allied with the Aztecs, and were more at ease at hearing of the hostility between them and the priests of Tetzapotitlan.

Again, Fra Angelico and Mahari walked with the native warriors, talking and gesturing and learning as much as they could as they descended from the mountains into the big valley. Again, crowds of people ran out to meet them, calling out in their language and curiously touching the stranger's armor and equipment as they passed.

They were afforded domed huts of thatch and timber whose floors were inset several feet below the surface of the ground. The timbers were pinned with wooden pegs and tied with rough woven rope and sealed with clay wattle.

Venison and trout spiced with sage and wild garlic and served with piping hot maize tortillas, squash, and yams were served on patterned ceramic dishes with wild geometric patterns. The hungry men devoured the food with aplomb, and eyed the women a little too hungrily.

After the meal, the Captain, Rico, Fra De La Cruz, Fra Angelico, and Mahari were led to the hut of the elders, where they sat upon rough woven mats upon the floor and smoked herbs through a long-stemmed wood and soapstone pipe.

The elders demanded to hear their tale from the beginning, and they did so with the aid of Mahari, using a combination of Nahuatl and a more universal native sign language. Over the course of many hours, they talked at length of the cities of Cibola, and the Aztec migration.

Kokopelli, they said, still came to their villages every year with goods from the Aztec Empire: bright feathers and worked gold jewelry which were exchanged for flint, elk horn and ivory, and bison hides. In this way they got news from far to the south and north, as Kokopelli made his yearly rounds.

The Aztecs, they said, were a breakaway group of Ute zealots, who had fled from the eastern and western Thunderbird mountain tribes. The two tribes had been at war with one another since the ascension of Huizilopotle to chiefdom of the western tribe.

It was he who claimed that Quetzalcoatl had appeared to him in the caves of Thunderbird Mountain and set upon the people a new religion of human sacrifice and extreme piety which was rejected by the eastern tribe.

The daughter of Huizilopotle rebelled and went to the lakes on the flanks of the mountain to bathe, where she was attacked by the Thunderbird for her transgression. The son of the chief of the eastern tribe saw the attack, and shot the thunderbird in the eye with a sling stone, blinding it and driving it away.

Then the two began to meet in secret, he bringing with him six great warriors, and she six beautiful handmaidens. They went to Thunderbird Mountain, each couple finding within a separate cave a refuge wherein they each bore seven sons and seven daughters. When these children came to adulthood, they set forth from their caves to travel south and conquer.

Seven times they conquered other great tribes as they went south, and each time did they build a city of gold, led by one of the founding seven clans. At a great lake in the mountains far to the south the descendants of Huizilopotle conquered a final tribe and become Lords of the Aztec Empire.

"Where is Thunderbird Mountain?" asked Fra De La Cruz as the night wore into dawn. The question was relayed in Nahuatl and sign language by Mahari.

The elder sage replied in kind, saying, "North beyond the mountains, follow the river upstream to the west to its source. Down the river beyond lies the Great Mountain of the Thunderbird. The Thunderbirds have flattened off the top of the mountain for their aerie, and the Caves of the Ancestors lay just below the top, guarded by the great Thunderbirds."

"Where did they mine the gold for the cities of Cibola?" asked Fray De La Cruz in turn.

"They take the gold from this mountain and that, as Quetzalcoatl provide for them with the light of the sun he has hidden in the stone." replied the elder.

"Are any such sites nearby?" De La Cruz asked again.

The sage replied, "Yes, in the Mountain of Demons Quetzalcoatl left his gold, guarded by demons of flashing light and the shadows that walk."

De La Cruz's eyes flashed in the flickering firelight as he asked, "Where is the Mountain of Demons?"

The sage replied again, "The Mountain of Demons is at the north end of this valley, near the point of a promontory marked by a great cross."

Now De La Cruz's shark's smile flashed with his eyes as he said, "You must lead us there, to the Mountain of Demons. Our God grants us mighty magic over such demons, and has marked the mountain with His symbol." De La Cruz withdrew his cross from where it hung beneath his shirt upon a chain. He held it up commandingly, the gold flashing in the firelight.

"It is given to us by God," continued De La Cruz, "that we should find the Caves of Quetzalcoatl and drive out the serpents, as we did in Tetzapotitlan." He looked piercingly at each of the others in the firelit hut in turn while holding aloft the cross and watching their reactions intently. "Those who aid us will find great reward, while those who oppose his will face death and an eternity of torment."

The elders talked among themselves for some time, and Mahari was able to translate little of what was said. At last the elder sage said, "What you say to us may be true, only the Gods can know. What you say also sounds very much like the words of the people of Huizilopotle as they came south to conquer. We will show you the Mountain of Demons, though we warn you that those who go there find only death and sorrow."

With the sunrise, they were led back to their huts, where they rested through much of the day. They rose and the command group met again in Captain Abetta's hut to plan the expedition to the Mountain of Demons.

In the end, it was decided that Fray De La Cruz would lead the party to the mine with Rico and Nahara and half the men, armed with two cannons. The others would remain in the village with the elders, awaiting word from the exploration party. Hymie was assigned to act as courier and scout as needed.

The party set out at dawn the next day, travelling north through the valley, at first along trails beside the fields of maize, squash, beans, yams, and potatoes. As they left the fields behind, great dunes of sand towered to their right at the foot of steep snow-capped mountains with a deep red hue.

"This is like unto the sands of the Moorish desert in Africa," said Fra De La Cruz, "though the dunes there extend as far as the eyes can see in every direction."

Rico nodded, silently looking from the dunes to Fray De La Cruz.

"Thanks be to God that these savages have no iron or steel weapons and armor." added Federico, "The Moors were a much deadlier enemy."

"Indeed," agreed Fray De La Cruz, "Mohammed was a warrior prophet, and he rewarded his men with the lands and property and wives and daughters of his enemy to inspire them to fight fiercely. Those who would convert were made to serve, and those who would not were made to pay a tax and thus serve as well. Those who did not serve were put to the sword, and their wives and daughters made to serve in the harem or die."

"Sounds like your interpretation of the encomienda." said Rico quietly.

Fray De La Cruz just smiled his shark's smile and rode on, as Federico chuckled softly.

They rode on through the day, and set camp in sight of the white stone cross high atop a spur of the dark red mountains. Throughout the evening, clouds raced up the valley, settling over the mountains. By nightfall the lightning flashed in the sky, lighting the cross and silhouetting the jagged ridgeline like an irregular strobe.

The native kept to themselves, watching the strangers warily with wide eyes and quick furtive gestures. They eyed the mountain and each flash of lightning as they efficiently set up a lean to on the lee side of a hill in which they all huddled beside a small campfire.

Dawn was grey as the sun rose vague and dim, and clouds completely obscured the eastern mountains with the spur and cross. The rain continued, soaking the party as they assembled for the climb up the rocky slopes. Hymie was sent ahead to scout, and he did so reluctantly in the dreary mist. The natives refused to proceed any further, merely pointing to the cross and lightly wooded drainage along the flanks of the ridge.

The others proceeded more slowly and carefully, plodding through the slippery mud of the valley floor until they reached the rocky talus and vegetated riparian woodland along the small stream at the foot of the promontory.

All day they climbed and plodded up the steep, rocky, and wet slopes through sparse pinon and juniper forest, then struggling through thick scrub oak along rough game trails. In turn the scrub gave way to aspen groves, then thick pines which at last diminished to alpine tundra. As they rose, so too the rain gave way to sleet and then wet, heavy snow.

Still they could not see the cross through the mist, and they set camp again, starting a fire in the shelter of a rocky shelf of red stone. All were soaked and weary, and they silently ate their cold rations of cornbread and venison jerky.

At length, Hymie returned from the mists ahead, his body seeming to smoke as the heat of his body evaporated the cold rain. He panted for a few moments from exertion before beginning his report.

"There is a cave, or mine portal," he said, "perhaps a quarter mile ahead and 400 feet above. The rocks there are painted with bizarre demon men and serpents." He took a few more deep breaths before continuing, "I did not go in the cave, and could not see how far it goes."

De La Cruz smiled and asked, "Did you see any tracks or evidence of habitation?"

"No, Fra De La Cruz." replied Hymie, "There are no people up there."

They spent a miserable, cold, and wet night in the freezing alpine storm huddled in tattered cloaks and bedrolls around the sputtering, smoky little fire beneath the towering cliffs and slopes. Still they rose at dawn and resumed the trek.

Another hour of plodding and climbing the wet, snowy, rocky slopes put them at the base of a shelf of light colored granite, the white cross upon the mountain, though any resemblance to a cross was lost from their perspective.

Beneath the white cliffs lay a heavily mineralized zone of mottled grey stone with a box-work of lighter red stone. A dark, roughly hewn shaft led some unknown distance into the mountainside and a pile of snow-covered tailings marked the entrance.

At the entrance to the mine, the troupe rested as guards were posted and a lantern was unpacked from their gear. Fray De La Cruz took up the lantern flanked by Anton, ordering Rico and Hymie to lead the way into the mine.

The lantern made dancing giants of their shadows on the rough walls of the shaft ahead as Rico and Hymie advanced with weapons drawn into the gloom. Less than one hundred feet ahead the adit opened into an irregular oval chamber with bands of orange, black, and yellow marking the walls. Over this dripped curtains of alternating white and grey limestone, which seemed to form bird's nests and pools at the base of the walls.

At the center of the room stood a block of limestone set with a patterned ceramic bowl filled with something unrecognizable with several pouches and a pipe. Arrayed about the block like the spokes of a wheel were six elongate mounds of limestone which resolved into lime-crusted skeletons at their approach.

Partially mummified in the thin dry air, the bodies wore dry rotted leather headdresses, shirts, pants, and moccasins, all adorned with feathers and beads of turquoise, malachite, silver, and gold. They wore rings, bracelets, and pendants of gold and silver as well, though all were crusted with calcification like a glaze of translucent wax.

"It appears we have found our mine." said Fray De La Cruz. "Hymie, you will return to the village and summon Captain Abetta and the village elders." He smiled his sharks smile again, lit eerily from below by the orange lamplight before continuing, "They will see that the demons of the mountain are nothing to men of God."

Hymie looked at De La Cruz for a moment, face impassive before he turned to descend the mountain again.

De La Cruz and Rico watched Hymie as he moved down the steep slopes for several minutes while the rest of the party rested. Then De La Cruz turned to Rico. "What did you do before you were conscripted for this voyage?"

"Caballero, Fra." replied Rico.

"I should have guessed from your skill with the horses." said De La Cruz, nodding. "Any of the boys do any mining?"

"I wouldn't know, Fra." said Rico. "Maybe Gonzales or Barres."

With a sharp grin De La Cruz said, "Well, you are all miners now, at least until we conscript some native workers. Gather the men, but set a watch. Let me show you boys what to look for."

Rico set two guards to watch and assembled the men at the mine entrance. De La Cruz strode to the front of the group and said, "See how the stone is fractured and altered below this sill of granite?"

The men grumbled and nodded in affirmative, and De La Cruz continued, "Notice the yellow, almost powdery substance coming from the altered area. What does it look like to you?"

The men shuffled their feet or looked around to avoid answering, so Rico spoke up, "It looks like rust, Fra."

"Indeed," said De La Cruz, "it is rust, iron oxide with other metals, and it is a sign of metal ore. The prospectors call it shine, and it points the way to the ore. Get me a lantern, chisel, and hammer."

When the lantern was brought to him and lit, De La Cruz led the men into the portal. He carefully walked along the walls, scanning the rock and picking at bits of it with a chisel. "Here." he said at last, "Give me the hammer."

He chiseled loose a few good chunks of layered rock and brought them out to the fireside. Then he picked about the talus, hefting a big slab of stone with a relatively flat face on top which he also brought to the fireside. Then he proceeded to crush the chunks of ore from the mine with the hammer and pick through the powdery remains. From the crushed stone he retrieved a few small flakes of gold, which he held up with a grin.

"This," he said, "will be the means to assure our place as lords of this land." He paused and looked down at the approach from the valley as he said, "Set the cannon to cover the approach, and keep it loaded and at the ready. Stay alert and ready with the arquebus as well. We'll show them our own Demons of the Mountain."

De La Cruz picked at the powdered stone a bit more, then said, "Get me a flat pan and some water." The soldiers stared at him blankly for a moment and he clarified, "A shallow cooking pan, to show you how to pan for gold."

The pan was quickly retrieved, and De La Cruz scraped a bit of the powdered stone into the pan, adding water and swirling the mixture to suspend as many particles as possible. Then he decanted off the water with much of the lighter minerals, repeating the steps until just a few bits of black minerals and a tiny bit of flaky gold was left.

He carefully extracted the gold flakes and dumped the remaining minerals before passing the pan to Rico. "Now you try it." he said.

Rico took his turn at panning, passing the pan to Sandoval when he became adept enough to recover a bit of gold. In turn, all the men learned to pan for gold, though many lacked the patience or diligence to do it well.

The next three days were spent laboring at the mines and learning primitive mining and smelting methods from Fray De La Cruz. By the third evening they had amassed a few ounces of gold, and some copper and tin, as well as a big pile of rejected rock and pulverized stone.

As the sun disappeared behind the mountains across the valley, the lookout called down, "The Indians are approaching with Captain Abetta."

"Take up your positions!" shouted De La Cruz. "Be ready for my command."

Rico looked sidelong at De La Cruz, "Surely you do not intend to attack them. Hymie and Captain Abetta are with them."

De La Cruz grinned sharply at Rico. "Just a precaution in case they become uncooperative.", he said as he began walking toward the mine approach.

Rico stared hard at De La Cruz and followed along behind. At the landing where the steep slope gave way to the bench with the mine adit, De La Cruz and Rico waited out of the line of fire for the canon and arquebuses.

At the head of the winding column approaching from below, Hymie waved up at them. Rico and De La Cruz waved back, the latter with his shark's grin wide. A shiver of dread ran up Rico's spine and his smile failed as the column got closer and closer and he saw Nahana with the group. He did not see Fra Angelico or Mahari among them.

When the group was close enough to communicate effectively, De La Cruz hailed Abetta, "Captain, the mine has gold, as we hoped. We just need a few dozen natives to work the stone."

Captain Abetta nodded, breathing heavily with the exertion of the long climb. "We will make note of the location so that we can report it back to the Crown."

De La Cruz's grin faded to ice, and he said, "Tell the Indians that the Mountain Demons with strike down upon them with wrath if they do not provide workmen for the mine."

The approaching group looked up at De La Cruz with worry.

"Tell them, Nahana." repeated De La Cruz coldly.

Nahana looked up at De La Cruz and Rico for a moment, then spoke a few words quickly in Nahuatl. The Indians looked back and forth between Nahana and De La Cruz before the Chief spoke. Then all the Indians turned and began to descend back down the mountainside.

Rico, too, looked back and forth at De La Cruz and Nahana, and when He saw De La Cruz's eyes narrow, he shouted, "Run!" charging down the slope toward Nahana and the others. Nahana dove away from the group into the small ravine adjacent to their route.

Almost as soon as Rico shouted, De la Cruz lifted and dropped his arm toward the Indians. "Fire!", he screamed, and the roar of the cannon and arquebuses came immediately after. Time seemed to slow as the cannon fire blasted into the group below, hurling bodies in all directions.

A large chunk of stone spun up from the impact and thudded into Rico's forehead, exploding the world in red. Rico stumbled forward a few more steps at a faltering run, but the red faded to black and he fell forward to roll and slide into the ditch unconscious with the dead and dying.

Chapter 14: Slaves No More

Rico awoke slowly as his head lolled back and forth with the jolting motion of the litter behind the horse. He lay bundled to the litter with the bundles of gear and treasure, but he could look behind as well as to the left and right.

Two other men followed along behind the laden horses, trudging wearily along up a mountain path through a large meadow. Thick forest of Aspen covered the steeper hillsides to both sides, and a plume of dark smoke rose from the valley behind them.

He tried to call out to the men following the horse, but his throat was so dry that his croaking could not be heard over the wind and plodding hoofbeats. Soon he drifted away again into the darkness of sleep.

When he next awoke, he lay in his bedroll near a campfire. He lay silently for a few moments, listening for voices over the wind and the crackling fire. Indeed, he could hear Fray De La Cruz talking quietly with another nearby.

His heart raced with thrill as he heard the other voice, though he could not make out the words. Nahana lived, thank God! He tried again to listen to the conversation, but the voices were too quiet or distant to comprehend.

At last he struggled to sit up, rasping "Water!" as loudly as he could. Sure enough, though, De La Cruz and Nahana were alert, and within moments Nahana was kneeling at his side with a bag of water. Rico swallowed a few painful gulps as his parched throat regained its elasticity, then he hugged Nahana tightly.

"Thank God you're alive!" he croaked.

Nahana smiled tepidly, and her eyes told him that much had gone wrong. Rico glanced over her shoulder at De La Cruz, who stood behind her with his shark's smile and cold eyes. He lay back again, shutting his eyes and trying to remember what had happened.

Without opening his eyes, he asked, "How many of us made it out of the valley?"

"Nine," replied De La Cruz, "plus the girl." Rico heard two heavy footfalls as De La Cruz approached, continuing, "Do not try anything rash. Nahana has become quite useful to us. See to it that you don't cause her any undue difficulties."

Rico sat up again and opened his eyes, nodded silently before asking, "What of Captain Abetta and Fray Angelico?"

De La Cruz' smile twisted to a sneer, "The Indians killed them when they refused the encomiendo. We were forced to cut our losses and continue on toward Cibola"

Rico's jaw clenched as he tried to hide his anger and struggled to remain silent in the face of such an obvious lie. Nahana had sat back on her heels, and she looked back and forth between the two men as she read their expressions with apparent fear and worry.

In the end, Rico just clutched Nahana to him and let the grief and pain flow out as quiet sobs and tears.

"Remain stalwart, Enrico Amiduras," said De La Cruz passionately, "and you will be among the richest and most renown men in all the world. If your family were noble, you would be in good standing for governorship, but with the gold we have amassed, you may still have a chance."

De La Cruz smiled again, though it gave no comfort. "Eat and drink, then rest." said De La Cruz. "There will be more trials and hardship in the days to come, and you will need your strength back." De La Cruz turned away, saying, "Sleep well." as he walked to his own bedroll.

Nahana joined Rico in his bedroll as De La Cruz prepared his own. For a few moments, Rico shut the world away and it was only he and Nahana, warm flesh and comfort in a cold, miserable world. Quietly, as they lay together, Nahana told Rico of the events since his injury.

Hymie, she said, had escaped the cannon fire and arquebus shot to flee back into the forest. Captain Abetta died in the initial cannon fire, and De La Cruz assumed command of the remaining Spanish. Many of the Indians who had survived the cannon were rounded up and forced to work in the mines, but the Spanish ran low on food and ordered some Indians to retrieve supplies from the village with a Spanish escort.

The Indians and the escort had never returned, and in frustration, De La Cruz ordered the remaining Indians into the mine, blasting the entrance behind them with the cannon. Then the whole remaining party had fled north under repeated attacks from the angry tribe.

Soon the only sound was the quiet crackling fire and the soft moan of the wind and Rico thought of crawling out of his bedroll to stealthily creep over and slit De La Cruz' evil throat. Surely there has been enough killing, he thought. De La Cruz had shown Nahana and he mercy back at the mine, and now Rico must also be merciful. At peace again, Rico slept.

For two more weeks, they traveled north and west, over many mountains and high valleys. The streams, which had flowed south and east as they climbed, now flowed largely west as they found themselves descending again. Where they could, they followed the stream courses to ensure an easy water supply in the high desert valleys and canyons.

As they had climbed higher into the mountains, snowstorms and winter weather had slowed their progress, and they had been forced to wait huddled in the camp for several days as blizzards passed. Still game was plentiful, and the intensity of the storms and depth of snow began to decline as they descended the mountains again.

They followed a river down a high, flat, sagebrush covered snowy valley where the river plunged into a trackless narrow canyon gorge. Thick, dark pine forests covered the slopes at the end of the valley on both sides of the gorge, and they elected to stay on the north rim.

Wherever they could, they stuck to game trails as they wound their way down the rugged mountainside. Several times, they were forced to retrace their steps as the game trails faded away or led to impassable slopes or cliffs. Eventually the black timber gave way to thinner Aspen groves again and they followed a ridgeline westward.

They descended yet further as the Aspen groves gave way to scrub oak and serviceberry, and they finally caught sight of the legendary flat-topped Mountain of the Great Eagles. Just as they had been told, the wide mountain loomed over the surrounding hills and valleys, snow-capped and flanked, but with a ring of dark cliffs at the top.

The snowy flanks of the mountain were broken into fantastic shapes by the uneven forestation and topography, and the shapes of giant white eagles could easily be imagined in the huge patches of snow. Still ahead and below them, two river valleys met in a wide, grey, shale valley where the snow had melted from the areas not sheltered from the sun.

Several plumes of light smoke were visible to the south and west in the valleys, and they knew that they would soon encounter more Indians.

Still, it took them two more days to reach the foot of the mountain, and they struggled through deep, sticky mud for much of the distance. They were forced to make many stops to clean the heavy mud from their feet, the horse's hooves, and the litter before they could continue plodding on.

At the confluence of the rivers, a camp sprawled in the grassy floodplain near the riparian cottonwood forest. Several dozen teepees surrounded a central area with an open fire, and a group of twenty or so warriors came out to meet them, clad in leather and bearing spears, stone axes, and bows.

They surrounded the group, eyeing them suspiciously until Nahana spoke to them in Nahuatl. "We are travelers from far to the south." she said. "We have journeyed very far to see the great mountain of our ancestors as was foretold."

The warriors' eyes widened at Nahara's assertion, and they chatted back and forth among themselves in an unfamiliar dialect of Nahuatl too quickly for even Nahana to understand. Then the warriors beckoned for the strangers to follow them, and they were led to the largest of the teepees. There Nahana, Rico, and De La Cruz were invited to enter.

Inside, a chief awaited with his wife and a venerable old woman around a small fire. They were invited to sit, and offered venison jerky and dried serviceberries before the chief spoke.

"What do you seek at the Sacred Mountain?" he asked. By this time, both De La Cruz and Rico had learned enough Nahuatl to understand, though neither could speak it well.

"We seek the caves of the ancestors," said De La Cruz clumsily.

"Why would you seek the caves of the ancestors?", asked the chief. "The living are not welcomed by the mountain, which is guarded by great eagles and the spirits of the dead."

The visitors looked back and forth between themselves, and De La Cruz answered, "We have come to pay our respects to the spirits and ask for their guidance."

Then the old woman spoke up, "You will find nothing but toil and death on that mountain, travelers. The great eagles will carry you away and your souls will remain in the spirit world for seven lifetimes."

The chief looked at the old woman, then back at the visitors. "You may rest here, and partake of our food and drink, but then you must go before the spirits see you with us and tie us to your fate." The chief gestured toward the tent flap, and they rose and exited the teepee.

From then on, none of the Indians in the camp would look at their faces, though they were given a teepee, food, and water. They rested that day, and the next, before moving on to the west along the south flank of the Grand Mesa.

Chapter 15: Redoubt

"We will set up a redoubt along the first major creek we come to leading up into the mountain." said De La Cruz. "There we can wait out the winter, safe from the Indians, should they turn on us again."

They traveled all that day and camped again along a tiny trickle of a stream. The next morning, they came upon a bigger creek flowing south from the mountain across the hilly grey shale foothills and peneplain toward the river canyon to the south.

This creek they followed north as the grey shale hills rose about them until they neared the snow-line and the beginning of the scrub forests above. There, at a point where the small valley narrowed between the hills, they set camp again.

In the days and weeks to follow, they gathered the black, vesicular basalt rocks which were the only good stone available, cut timber from the cottonwoods, hunted, fished, and dried meats to keep them fed through winter.

Each hunting trip also doubled as a scouting trip for the ancestral caves, although the expeditions did not proceed very far up the mountain in the deepening snow. Soon, caves were reported, though none showed signs of mining or habitation beyond some smoke staining of the walls and ceilings.

In a lull between storms, De La Cruz led the horses laden with the treasure-filled litter to the best of the caves, where he and Rico buried the treasure beneath an overhanging shelf of rock. They walled up the rest of the hollow with flagstone and covered the façade with earth, blending it into the surroundings as best they could.

De La Cruz began work on a map of their travels, noting important locations as best he could with just a compass and estimated distances. Frequently, scouts and lookouts saw Indians watching them or the camp from afar, but the scouts could never catch them when attempts at contact were made.

As winter dragged on, the food began to run low. Snow had piled up deep against the walls of the redoubt, and bitter cold settled in. Months of close quarters and poor conditions had the men on edge, and many still resented Nahana and Rico's marriage and wanted her for themselves.

Rico took Nahana with him to hunt whenever he could, as much to keep her safe from the men as for her excellent help on the hunt. Raised as she was on the shores of the Caribbean, she hated the snow and bitter cold, and would remain behind on the coldest days.

On one such occasion, Rico heard her screams as he neared the redoubt. He hurried back to the redoubt, bursting in to see Barres holding Nahana down as Gonzales had his way with her. Rico sprang forward as he drew his sword, driving the point straight through Gonzales' back.

Barres leapt back, grabbing for his arquebus, but Rico slashed his throat with the sword and he staggered back spurting blood as he clutched at his neck.

Then De La Cruz stepped in from his chamber, firing his own gun. The blast missed Rico as he lunged at Barres, hitting Nahana as she pushed Gonzales' body off her and struggled to rise. Rico spun and leapt at De La Cruz, slashing again with the sword.

De La Cruz blocked with his gun, and the sword cut into the wooden stock deeply. De La Cruz charged forward, knocking Rico into the table where Gonzales slumped atop Nahara on the rough wood table. Down in a heap went De La Cruz and Rico atop the bodies and splintering table.

Rico rolled backward, kicking at De La Cruz as he did, and flipping De La Cruz into the stone walls upside-down. De La Cruz crashed into the ground, rolling to his side and swinging the broken arquebus like a club to thud into Rico's back and shoulders.

Rico pressed forward, trying to stab at De La Cruz with the sword, but unable to get a good angle with the long weapon. Rico dropped the sword and clutched at De La Cruz's throat, crushing the larynx with a thumb. De La Cruz struggled mightily, gurgling and writhing as he tore at Rico's strong fingers.

Still Rico clamped his hands even tighter as De La Cruz turned redder and redder in the face and finally collapsed unmoving. For long moments Rico held the dead man by the throat as he looked into Nahana's eyes and saw the light of consciousness leave them for the last time.

With tears in his eyes he held her body to him for a long moment. Then he rose again, looking about wildly. He strode into De La Cruz's chamber, dug through his gear, and seized the scroll case with the map and letters.

Then he ran back out into the cold, saddling the horse as quickly as possible and gathering his bedroll and gear. As soon as he finished, he climbed into the saddle and began trotting back to the south with the only other surviving horse in tow.

Shouting arose behind him, and he spurred the horse on faster. Then came the booming of the arquebus, and he felt the bullet tear into his back. He rode on through the pain, following the creek to the river, which he forded on the horse.

Another creek flowed into the river from the south not far away, and he followed its steep canyon on to the south all that day. He slept fitfully and shivering through the night, and continued on at first light. All through the next day, and the next again he rode on and on and on as delirium took him.

Then he found himself walking, plodding, really as he faded in and out of reality. About him was nothing but dust and pain, and he wandered in and out of his memories scattered and lost.

There, ahead he saw green trees and sunshine, and Nahana was there waiting for him. He smiled through his parched lips as he ran to her, though he stumbled and fell.

Then the trees were gone, Nahana was gone, and the desolation surrounded him again. He crawled under a small shelf of rock and rolled to his back, the scroll case still clutched in his fingers. He could almost feel Nahana holding him tight, almost feel her warm breath on his cheek.

"It is as the old woman said." he thought. "We are but ghosts, lost in the dust of this new land."

The chill of the desert night sunk into Lily as she lay in the dirt below the ledge. Then suddenly a warm, soft kiss brushed against her cheek and nuzzled her neck. "A nice dream!" she thought as the darkness pulled at her. Then the nuzzling came again, and with it a familiar nicker: Redwing had found her!

Act III: Chapter 16: Nice

Everything was warm and soft, and a diffused golden light enveloped her as her senses slowly returned. Then there was the delicious scent of bacon and coffee through the smell of clean linen. At last, feminine humming and light, distant singing.

"Heaven!" she thought. "This must be heaven."

As she basked in rare comfort, she slowly came to realize that the voice, though slightly familiar, was not that of her Mother. Her battered head and abraded body ached badly, and her stomach grumbled with hunger, and she knew it was not Heaven, though it sure was nice.

Then came the sound of stairs creaking under measured footfalls and a door opening, so she opened her eyes and sat up. In walked her neighbor, Mrs. Chisholm, with a tray laden with bacon and eggs, pancakes with butter and syrup, glasses of water and juice, and a steaming cup of coffee.

"Good morning, Miss DuCray." said Mrs. Chisholm as she walked to the bedside with the tray. "You are in some terrible trouble, my Dear, but I don't believe a word of what the Sherriff and your Brother, Ben say about you. No girl who takes such good care of horses could be half as bad as that."

She set the tray in Lily's lap and walked across the room to the dresser, picking something up from the shelf and returning.

"You had this thing clutched in your hand when your horse brought you half-dead through our yard. Sam brought you in just as they were talking about Jake's killing on the news. Sherriff Sandborn said you stole Jake's gun and shot him and three men down at the Miner's Luck."

Lily drank the water down in a few gasping gulps as she listened, then grabbed up a piece of bacon, chomping off a bite. "Thank you, Mrs. Chisholm!", exclaimed Lily, "You saved me! I would be dead if Ben or the Sherriff caught me. Jake killed my Mom, and Ben tried to rape me! I shot Jake and tried to run away, but Ben wrecked us and took the gun."

She gulped down the half-chewed bacon, and continued, "Jake must have shot the men who tried to protect me at the bar. I don't know how Redwing found me, but he saved me, too. Why did you hide me and take care of me?"

"Any fool could see you would get no justice from Sherriff Sandborn and company." said Mrs Chisholm. "Jake and Ben are both rotten to the core, but I doubt you can afford a lawyer good enough to convince a Judge and Jury of that."

Lily ate hungrily again, chasing the food with coffee and orange juice as Mrs. Chisholm continued, "Sam put Redwing in the stables out of sight, and he's headed into Grand Junction tomorrow with the horse trailer for supplies. We could put Redwing up at the Fischer's place in Kannah Creek for the time being until we can get this sorted out."

Mrs. Chisholm lifted the scroll case again, asking, "What is this thing anyway? It sure looks old."

"I don't know, Mrs. Chisholm.", replied Lily. "I think it might be Spanish, from the Conquest, but I don't know. I had the longest, most vivid dreams about a Conquistador while I was passed out in the desert. I think it could be an important relic."

"Sam can take you by the Museum." said Mrs. Chisholm. "They have quite an exhibit of Spanish artifacts from the Age of Conquest. Maybe you could ask the Curator about it tomorrow."

"I picked up some new clothes for you at the Mercantile." said Mrs. Chisholm as she walked back to the dresser and opened a drawer. "I hope you like them. I think you'll be really pretty in these, though they are much more modest than those poor, shredded rags you had on when we found you."

Lily was suddenly conscious that she was naked beneath the blankets, and she pulled the sheet up over her breasts before finishing the last of her meal.

"How are you healing up?", asked Mrs. Chisholm.

"My whole body aches," replied Lily, "but I feel way better now with my full tummy and a cup of warm coffee. Thank you so very much, Mrs. Chisholm. You are an angel."

"It's nothing, Dear.", said Mrs. Chisholm. "I'm sure you would do the same for us if we needed it. You've always seemed to be a very nice young person, despite what the teenyboppers and fuddy-duddies say about you. You're an individual, and they can't stand that."

"You'll have to be careful, your name and an old picture are all over the news.", continued Mrs. Chisholm. "The new clothes will help, and I'll help you do something different with your hair when you get out of the shower. We'll also fix you up with some makeup to hide all those bruises and scratches."

"Thanks again, Mrs. Chisholm." said Lily with a sated smile.

"You're welcome, Dear." Mrs. Chisholm replied. "The shower and bathroom are down the hall, first door to the left. Come on down when you get cleaned up. Redwing will be happy to see you."

She showered and joined the Chisholms downstairs as requested, and they chatted all through dinner, as she told them of her adventure and dream about the conquistador. Soon after supper, her battered body was tired, and she went to bed early.

The next morning, she rose at dawn and dined on eggs, bacon, and pancakes again before helping Sam load Redwing onto the horse trailer. They did not notice the Sherriff in his white SUV watching from the parking lot of the Miner's Luck as they pulled out onto Highway 141 toward Grand Junction.

Chapter 17: Ages Past

The aged volunteer Receptionist at the museum gladly showed Lily the way to the Spanish Colonial display area of the museum. She explained that some of the artifacts and accompanying information were the result of an archaeological expedition to the Kannah Creek area.

Before the old lady could walk away back to her post near the gift shop, Lily asked, "I was wondering if the Curator is in today?"

The Receptionist turned slowly back to Lily as she said, "Yes, I believe Mr. Dunbury is in. Why do you ask?"

Lily pulled the scroll case out of her new purse, saying, "I found this out in Dry Creek Basin, and I thought it might be a Spanish artifact of some sort."

The old lady eyed the scroll case with interest, and said, "I'll let him know you're here.", before waddling back to her post.

In the cases Lily saw a swivel cannon, cuirass, pike, and morion, all reproductions or imported relics, but very similar to those she had seen in her dream. The gun, however, was and exact replica of one of the arquebus from her dream, and pieces of such a gun, according to the placard on the display cabinet, were found in the ruin of a suspected redoubt near Kannah Creek.

The hair at the nape of her neck crept as she recalled her vivid dream, and just then, she felt a tap upon her shoulder. She screamed and jumped, which in turn startled the Curator, who leapt back from her into one of the displays.

"Sorry to startle you, Miss." said the balding, slightly pear-shaped Curator. "I'm Miles Dunbury, the Curator here at the Museum of the West."

He extended his hand, and Lily laughed at her fright, taking his hand and saying, "Sally Myers, pleased to meet you."

"I hear you found something you'd like to have me take a look at." he said.

"Yes," said Lily, "I found this way out in Dry Creek Basin under a ledge with some crumbled bones and rusted metal." She handed him the scroll case, adding, "I thought you might know what this is."

His eyes widened with excitement as he carefully turned the item over in his hands, studying it intently. "We shouldn't even be handling this without gloves.", he mumbled, before continuing louder, "This looks like a Bishop's scroll case from maybe fifteenth or sixteenth century Spain. The brass metal is quite corroded, and the iron is completely oxidized and fused, but it still may well be sealed."

Dunbury looked up from the relic, saying, "Would you allow me some time to look at this and do a little more research? If you don't mind, I'd like to try to open it. I can't guarantee that there won't be any damage, but I'll try to keep it to the minimum possible."

She nodded, and mumbled, "Yes, I ..."

Before she could finish her sentence, he continued, "Is there a number where I can reach you? Do you live here in the valley?"

"Sorry, I don't have a phone," she said, "and I have no place safe I can really go."

He looked back up at her briefly with wide eyes over the rims of his glasses, "Are you in some kind of trouble?"

She looked back at him with a panicky glance, explaining, "Abusive family, I'm under a protection order, but if my ex finds me, I don't know what he might do."

Again, he looked up at her over the rims of his glasses, saying, "I'm afraid it may be a little boring for you while I work on this, but you're welcome to stay for now. There is a lot to learn here, though, if you're interested." He smiled widely as he continued, "and you can always volunteer."

"I want to know everything I can learn about the scroll case and Kannah Creek site." said Lily.

"Me too!" said the Curator excitedly.

As they walked to the front of the museum where Miles introduced Lily to Molly Lindstrom, the volunteer receptionist. Then they took the stairs to the basement, which was stacked to the walls with cryptically marked boxes and antique furniture.

Within the labyrinthine depths Miles led them to his office, which was also stacked with goods and papers. He gathered a reference book and file of notes from his desk before handing the folder to Lily and sitting in his worn office chair.

"That is my copy of the notes from this last summer's field expedition to the Kannah Creek site." he said. "The land owner brought in the first few artifacts, just as you did. It was just a few musket balls, and bits of metal, but we managed to match the metal bits to parts from an old Spanish pistol, which you may have seen upstairs."

"Since then we have found more parts of Spanish origin, roughly dated to the early to mid-sixteenth century." He continued, "All of this brings Spanish explorers here almost forty years earlier than was originally thought."

Then there was silence for some hours, as each poured over the volumes at hand, accounts of Spanish explorers and archeological and historic records.

At length Miles arose and said, "I am taking this to the lab. First, we'll clean it up a bit, and re-examine it for markings. Then we'll have a go at opening it. A little WD-40 goes a long way. You're welcome to come along and help if you like."

"Thanks for being so nice to me." she said, "People aren't usually very nice to me, but everybody I've met in the last few days has been really nice. Thank you again."

"Oh, that's quite alright." said Curator Dunbury. "We're all pretty nice around here. "It's very nice to see a young person so interested in ages past."

The lab was nearly as cluttered as the rest of the non-public areas of the museum, but the work space on one of the benches was clear, so he set the scroll case down there. He donned surgical gloves and applied a solvent to a rag, which he used to rub and pick at the scale and dirt covering the scroll case. Then he examined it with a hand lens. "This is the blazon of Bishop Fonseco, about 1511 or so."

He put down the hand lens and applied some WD40 to the seal at one end of the tube. A little excess ran down the side of the tube and he wiped it up with a paper towel. Then he twisted the tube back and forth. Bits of the iron closure clasp fell away in clumps of rust, then the top of the tube twisted and Dunbury pulled it off.

He carefully dumped the contents out on the lab counter, tugging gently on the thin, rolled leather within. His hands shook as he very gently unrolled the leather and parchments hidden within. With equal care he flattened all the documents and began to carefully examine them each in turn.

"My God!" he said, "This appears to be an original copy of the Encomiendo of 1511, signed by Bishop Fonseco himself! How on earth did this document get to an overhang in western Colorado?"

He moved the letter to the side, and looked at the next, which included letters of commendation for Fray Benito De La Cruz to lead an expedition with fellow friars Dominic Angelico and Ronaldo Estevan. There were three ships, from Lisbon on June 23, 1511 bound for the New World via Cuba. He laid this carefully aside.

Beneath was a Letter from Queen Isabela of Spain ordering the arrest of Fray Montesino for apostatism.

Last was a hand drawn map of the east coast of North and Central America, along with notes and a plotted course up the Rio Grande and beyond to a clear depiction of the Grand Mesa.

Dunbury sat back stunned, staring across the desk at Lily, who became suddenly very uncomfortable beneath his gaze. "These documents are priceless!" he said, "To think that you just found these in the desert… Amazing."

"We've got documented proof that the expedition really did build a redoubt on Kannah Creek in 1511 or shortly thereafter." He shook his head in astonishment. "Can you take me to the site?"

"Maybe," she said, "but I was lost at the time I found them with the bones and metal." She looked into his expectant eyes and shied away. "Perhaps there is enough detail on the map."

She stood and peered down at the map with Dunbury for a few moments.

"This," he said, "is the Rio Grande running up to Taos before there was a Taos." He pondered a few more seconds and continued, "So this must be the San Luis Valley."

"Then this is the Gunnison River Valley." said Lily, pointing, "and the confluence at Delta… and here is Kannah Creek!"

"Indeed!" agreed Dunbury excitedly, "and here is the redoubt, right here on the map!"

"Then what is this?" asked Lily, pointing to a mark and series of notes on the flanks of the Grand Mesa not far from the redoubt.

"I have no idea," said Dunbury, shaking his head, "but I am dying to find out! I will call up the field team, first thing in the morning. They can get everything together while we look over Google Earth and plan the base camp location and best routes to the site."

Lily began to worry a bit, he continued, "I'll photograph and prepare the documents for further study and get a few of my colleagues to come in to examine them as well." She began shaking her head, but he kept on, "We'll call a press conference, and this will be world news in archaeological circles."

"No!" she cried suddenly, "Nobody can know about me at all! I, and anybody around me is in terrible danger if my stalker gets wind of me."

"Ok, it's ok!" said Dunbury, "We'll keep this whole thing quiet until we find a safe place for you to be. Maybe we can do a little preliminary investigation ourselves before we bring in anyone else."

He started his computer and pulled up the location of the Redoubt on Google Earth. Then they scrolled about on the screen, guessing at the location and the meaning of the cryptic markings.

"Here is Kannah Creek," he said, "which we can see on the map, and that is Indian Point."

"So that puts our X right in here along this cliff feature." explained Lily.

"Exactly!" agreed Dunbury. "We can get there via Kannah Creek Trail. Just a couple hours hike up."

"Or a forty-five minute horseback ride." said Lily.

"Do you have horses?" asked Dunbury.

"Just one," replied Lily, but he's up at a ranch on Kannah Creek already, so... maybe we could borrow another horse for you."

Dunbury touched the print icon, and the map began noisily printing on the printer atop the crowded workbench. "I'm really not that good with horses," he said, "but I'm willing to hike it."

"Tomorrow morning?" asked Lily.

"Seven thirty am sharp." Replied Dunbury.

"Perfect!" exclaimed Lily, "Can I sleep on your couch?"

Chapter 18: Killer at Large

Mrs. Dunbury proved to be a wonderful, if surprised hostess.

"Um, Miss Myers, this is my sweet wife, Sarah." said Miles. "Sarah, Darling, this is Sally Myers. She is a young historical enthusiast taking refuge from a violent ex-spouse."

"Very nice to meet you, Dear." said Sarah. "How is it that you came to my husband for refuge in this situation? It hardly seems the role of the Museum to shelter battered women."

Lily stammered, aghast, but Miles was un-fazed. "No, Darling, Miss Myers came to the museum today to share a spectacular Spanish Colonial find she had made. The drama is secondary to the situation."

Mrs. Dunbury shook her head sadly, "Come here, Miss Myers." she said. "There are some things a Lady just can't talk about with men." She extended her hand toward Lily. "Come, I have wine, and I am a very good listener."

She whisked Lily away to the kitchen, where she opened a bottle of *Colorado Cellars* Pinot Griggio and poured three glasses. "Let me go take this glass to Miles, and I'll be right back."

Mrs. Dunbury snatch up the glass of wine and went back to the living room where Miles had settled into a recliner and switched on the television. "Here, Darling, some wine for you." said Sarah.

The television came on, drowning out the rest of the conversation, but she caught the introduction of the local news. "Breaking news on the story out of San Miguel County of the shooting of Nucla resident Jake Vigil. The body of a woman believed to be Sherry DuCray, the mother of the under-age shooting suspect Lily DuCray was found in her wrecked car in the bottom of the Dolores River Canyon near the former town of Uravan, Colorado by local search and rescue personnel."

Lily gasped and started, turning to look toward the living room and spilling a little bit of her wine onto the counter and her blouse. In came Sarah, again, asking, "Is everything alright, Dear?"

Lily shook as she grabbed a paper towel from the roll on the dispenser atop the kitchen counter. As she dabbed up the spilt wine, she tried not to cry and hid her face, mumbling, "No, I'm fine," she said, "just a little embarrassed about spilling the wine."

"Don't you worry about the wine, dear." said Sarah. "I can see that you are in some pretty serious trouble, Sally. Miles and I would really like to help."

Lily shook like a leaf as she stammered, "I'm OK, really. Just tired and scared, is all. I just don't have anyone to turn to."

"You poor dear," said Sarah, "you are positively terrified." Sarah stepped up to Lily and embraced her against her ample bosom. At such close proximity, Sarah saw the terrible bruises and abrasions covering Lily from her ordeals. She shook her head sadly and said, "There, there, dear."

Like a burst pipe, Lily burst into sobbing tears, shuddering and incoherent as she sobbed in Mrs. Dunbury's arms. Miles rose and came into the kitchen in alarm at the emotional outburst, but Sarah turned him away with a glance and held Lily tight until the sobs faded away.

"You can tell me all about it." said Sarah, "I swear that none of this will get out to the authorities until we have a firm strategy to deal with the situation."

Lily nodded and told Sarah her story as they drank wine and snacked on crackers and cheese. Lily talked about the death of her father Sal and the trip to the ranch in Nucla. She talked about how the Ranch caretaker Jake had seduced and controlled her Mother, Sherry, and finally killed her. She even told about the shooting, and attempt to run to California, including the wreck and her recovery at the Chisholm's.

Throughout the story, Sarah remained supportive and sympathetic, commenting at the appropriate times and making sure the wine glasses were never left empty.

At long last, the tale was told, and Lily was exhausted from the outpouring emotions, the wine, and her mending body. Miles had already gone to bed and the house was quiet when Sarah finally led Lily to the guest bedroom, where she tucked Lily in and bid her goodnight.

At seven am, Miles knocked upon her door and announced, "Good morning, Sally. Time to get a move on and find out what our Fray De La Cruz marked on the map up Kannah Creek." She rose, dressed, and joined Miles in the kitchen, where he poured her a steaming cup of coffee and pointed her to the creamer and sugar bowl.

"Hopefully you are none the worse after a night drinking wine with Sarah." said Miles with a grin over the rim of his glasses.

Lily smiled sheepishly, "I feel pretty good, thanks."

"Excellent!" said Miles with a wink. "We've got some pretty steep, overgrown terrain to explore today, so I'm glad you don't feel too hung over."

"Me too!" said Lily. "Is Sarah coming with us?" she asked.

"No," said Miles, "field expeditions are not her cup of tea. She is sleeping in this morning. She says it is undignified to appear before nine am."

"I guess I'm not very dignified." said Lily.

"Nor am I," agreed Miles, "but I am lucky that she tolerates my lacking as well as she does."

"Your wife is a very sweet Lady." said Lily.

"Don't let her hear you say so," said Miles. "She has a reputation for fierceness she tries to uphold." He smiled again, adding, "She really is very sweet, though. Thank you."

Coffee cups in hand, they walked out to Miles' rather aged green Jeep Grand Cherokee. He thumbed the key fob to open the doors and they got in and secured their safety belts before backing out onto the residential street and pulling away.

They stopped at Carl's Jr. for breakfast sandwiches on the way out of town, which they had eaten by the time they pulled into the driveway of the Fischer Ranch off the Kannah Creek Road.

There, running back and forth along the fence line of the pasture was Redwing, and he stopped to snort at them and whinny when the Jeep was parked and they got out. Lily was already petting Redwing and stroking his jawline when Bob Fischer came out of the barn to greet them.

"Good morning!" said Bob when he saw Lily. "That horse sure is glad to see you."

Lily turned toward Bob, saying, "Good morning, Mr. Fischer. Thanks for keeping care of Redwing for me. I really appreciate it."

"No problem, young Lady." replied Bob before turning to Miles, extending his hand, and saying, "Bob Fischer, nice to meet you."

"Miles Dunbury," replied Miles, "and it's a pleasure to meet you as well."

"Are you taking Redwing out for a ride?" asked Bob.

"Yes," replied Lily, "We're headed up Kannah Creek Trail for a ways this morning."

"Be careful up there, there's been a bear hanging around." said Bob.

"Redwing and I ain't scared of any bear," said Lily, "but thanks for the heads-up."

"You campin' up there, or will you be back later today?" asked Bob.

"We brought gear for camping," replied Miles, "but with any luck we'll be back by the end of the day."

"It's still a little chilly up the mountain this time of year," said Bob, "but it should be decent camping weather."

"We'll just see how it goes." said Lily.

Soon Lily was trotting up the shoulder of Kannah Creek Road behind Miles in his Grand Cherokee. The Jeep cruised on ahead up the twisting roadway toward the trailhead, where Miles would try to get a head start hiking and Lily could catch up later, on Redwing.

Neither of them saw the big red pickup truck exit the pull-off along Reeder Mesa Road atop the adjoining flat ridgeline and head toward the intersection with Kannah Creek Road.

The trail began in an unoccupied, irregularly shaped gravel parking lot with a gate at the trailhead. For several miles, the trail traversed along the mountainside through sparse Pinon, Juniper, and Cedar forest, following along an irrigation canal for part of the way. Lily soon caught up to Miles as he trundled along with his heavy pack.

Lily walked Redwing slowly as they chatted for a bit along the way. "Be sure to stop and wait for me at the second Creek we come to." said Miles, joking, "We'll have to leave the trail at that point, so if we get lost, at least we'll be lost together."

"I'll wait." Lily assured him with a smile before riding on ahead at a walk.

As the elevation increased, the trail left the ditch behind, and scrub oak and serviceberry began to predominate. She crossed a rocky, tumbling stream choked with oak brush and nettles, and the trail meandered through groves of Aspen. The soft rustling and soughing soothed her, but she felt a sense of growing unease as she continued on.

The beauty of the forest calmed her as she rode. Beyond each of the Aspen groves was a meadow filled with an assortment of wildflowers in bright yellow, purple, blue, red, and orange in all different sizes and shapes. She startled a herd of elk as she broke out of a stand of trees, and she saw dozens of the huge, dark brown and tan animals bound away through the meadow and into the next stand of Aspen.

At length, she came upon a second stream, rolling and tumbling among the boulders and moss beneath the Aspens and pines. She dismounted and brushed Redwing for a long while as she chatted with him idly. "Where is he?" she asked at last.

Redwing whickered an answer, and Lily added, "Yes, we have been waiting a long time." She nuzzled his velvet nose with her own, and added, "I'm sure he'll be along soon enough."

Still he did not appear, so she walked through the forest around the stream crossing. There among the dank moss and moist black earth, she saw a clump of mushrooms growing. She plucked a few, examining them carefully and recalling memories of a wild mushroom book she had recently browsed. Certain that they were not toxic toadstools, Lily nibbled at one of the caps, and found it to be bland, but good tasting.

She sat in the grass and leaned wearily against a mossy boulder. Her body ached from injury and fatigue, and she was tired and a little hung over from staying up late drinking wine with Sarah. She munched idly on another mushroom and lay her head back for a moment, listening to the chirping of crickets and the soft drone of the mosquitos and bees.

Chapter 19: Dance of the Elves

The crickets, it seemed, had their own little melody, repeated over and over in a round, with the buzzing bees providing an accent. Soon she was sure she heard high, bright voices on the wind as well, and the whole thing seemed to fit together like music.

She opened her eyes, glancing drowsily around before her eyes snapped wide open at the sight. Faeries danced all around her as she lay back against the boulder along the creek. She smiled to herself and thought, "What a lovely dream."

The little, winged creatures flitting around her beckoned to her with tiny hands to follow them, and the music seemed to be fading away in the distance up the hillside. She rose, and the faeries scattered toward the sound of the music, looking back at her to see if she followed.

Up the hill through the trees she ran, chasing the giggling faeries and laughing at the absurdity of it. Then, in a small meadow at the heart of a thick stand of Aspen, she caught up to the Faeries.

They danced in a circle around a group of bizarre musicians, playing a wild assortment of improvised instruments and singing incomprehensibly in strange, high voices. Some played flutes of wood or upon reeds like an oboe. Some banged with sticks upon stones or wood, or scraped rough sticks together. Still others plucked at stringed instruments or blew on wooden horns, but somehow the whole made music, to which the faeries danced.

Into their midst came the loveliest of the elves, long golden hair billowing with motion in an unfelt wind. She sang beautifully, and though Lily did not understand any of the words, she got a sense of their meaning. Then she, too began to dance, slowly at first but building in intensity and tempo until the dance became a frenzy and the music a cacophony.

Then, as one, the faeries and their queen turned to Lily, seemingly spinning around her at an incredible rate. The music was gone, and all the voices whispered in an overlapping repeating chorus, "Wake up!"

Suddenly all was quiet again, with just the sounds of crickets and the burbling brook. Lily opened her eyes, still a bit disoriented from the wild dream as she lay back against the mossy boulder. Redwing grazed contentedly nearby, and he looked up at her and snorted when she moved.

The sense of dread overcame her, and she got up quickly. Miles should have arrived by then, and she worried about what might have happened to him. She grabbed the reins and led Redwing up the hillside through the thick forest toward the topographic features she had flagged on the map and satellite images, determined to find the site with or without the help of the Curator.

She picked her way through the trees to the base of a set of sandstone shelves and low cliffs and began comparing the features to those on the paper copy of the map she had brought along. At last she was fairly sure she had the right set of cliffs, so she began searching the sandstone ledges more thoroughly.

Several hours of this had her beginning to despair of finding anything there at all, when she saw a marking carved into the top of one of the sandstone shelves. She compared the mark to that on the map, and was excited to see that they matched. Still her sense of unease grew, and she shuddered at every noise as she began to dig below the shelf with the garden spade she had brought along.

A short time later she felt the spade hit something in the loose soil beneath the ledge. She scraped away earth from the object, which turned out to be one of several flagstones stacked below the ledge. She pried and pulled at the flagstones, removing them in turn and noting that the surface beneath was very flat and uniform.

At length, she found an edge of the object, and then another. Bits of rotten canvas came away with the spade, and beneath the canvas she saw metal-bound wood as she slowly unearthed a large chest.

When she had cleared enough soil away, she dragged the chest out from beneath the ledge and examined the latch. The iron bits of the latch had largely rusted into unrecognizable lumps of rust, and they broke away with a few twists, allowing her to open the lid. She gasped and fell back on her heels when she saw the array of golden treasure within.

Her nape rose as she gazed at the golden earrings, torques, bracelets, and ornaments she had seen in her dream from so long ago. There, too were the pieces of statuary of gold and jade from the tomb and temple. She picked up the obsidian mirror, and could almost see the dark reflection of the spurting bright blood in its surface.

Behind the chest beneath the ledge she found yet more items wrapped in disintegrating oil-cloth, but with growing alarm, she pushed the items back under the ledge. From the chest, she retrieved as much jewelry and smaller gold items as she could reasonably fit into her pack. Then she shoved the chest back beneath the ledge as well and recovered the lot with flagstones and dirt.

She carefully concealed the excavation site with dirt and rock before looking back down the slope past Redwing toward the trail. Redwing, too, was on alert, browsing here and there, but raising his head frequently to look around and cock his ears in various directions at the forest noise.

Chapter 20: Hard Road

When she was satisfied at the concealment of the treasure, Lily took up the reins and led Redwing back to the trail. She looked back and forth along the trail for signs of other traffic, but she saw no other human footprints besides her own.

Back down the trail she went, slowly at first, then more quickly as she began to fear for Miles. "What could have happened to him?" she thought. She imagined him falling and becoming injured, and envisioned him being attacked by a bear or mountain lion, so she watched carefully for any sign of struggle.

Back at the first of the creeks she had crossed on the way up the mountain, she dismounted and searched the exit point of the creek for signs of passage, and there she clearly saw two sets of men's footprints crossing the creek in both directions atop the hoofprints of her own earlier passage.

She recognized the size and pattern of the larger boot print. "Ben!" she muttered under her breath, "How in the hell did he find me?"

She remounted and hurried along the trail. "We've got to be really careful, Redwing." she said, "Ben has done something to Miles, I'm sure of it, but we can't let him use Miles to get at us."

Redwing nickered softly as if in agreement, and they rode on in wary silence.

At length, she heard voices ahead and she reined to a stop to listen.

"I'm afraid you've got the wrong guy, I have no idea what you are talking about." came Miles' voice, raised high and cracking with fear.

"Shut the fuck up, or I'w shoot you right here." Ben's clumsy voice growled through the trees. "I saw you dwop hew off at the wanch."

Lily shook with fear atop her horse at the sound of Ben's hateful voice, and it was a few moments before she could do anything. She thought about possible escape routes. Kannah Creek Trail ran some ten miles from the trailhead in the basin below to Carson Lake near the top, and several other trails joined in along its length.

None of the other trail spurs were near, though, and all of them would take her a great many hours to travel. She feared that Ben might well kill Miles before she could get anywhere to find help, and she wanted to do all she could to help him after his kindness to her.

There was another short spur, she remembered, very near the parking lot, which led down to a small park on the banks of the creek, and she thought she might be able to turn off there and get to a house along the road before Ben realized she had left the forest.

She rode along slowly, and as quietly as possible, listening for sounds ahead of her. When she reached the trail junction, she turned off toward the park and kicked Redwing into a gallop along the narrow trail. Redwing bound over the gate to the park, and a few seconds later, over the fence along the road.

Then Redwing's hooves rang loud upon the pavement as they raced up the switchback toward Reeder Mesa. Even over the sound of galloping hooves on the asphalt, they heard the roar of Ben's truck starting and the sound of churning gravel beneath his tires as he sped out of the parking lot, followed by a brief screech as the tires broke traction on the road.

"Run, Redwing!" she yelled, kicking her heels into his flank and sitting his back like a jockey. She turned off the road onto the first driveway she came to. Past the old ranch house she raced, and up the jeep trail beyond as it wound up the steep mountainside in a series of narrow switchbacks.

She still heard the roar of the engine as the truck sped past, and the sound off Ben's tires as he screeched to a halt just past the driveway and backed up to turn in as well. Then the roar of the engine grew nearer at an alarming rate. Still she raced up the jeep track, around another switchback, Redwing's heels kicking up clumps of sod as he slipped on the moist earth.

Then the trail ended at a closed mine shaft on a pile of overgrown coal mine tailings. She reined Redwing in and turned back, as the red Dodge raced around the last switchback toward her. Just as the truck came into the clearing in front of the mine, she spurred Redwing back down the trail.

The truck turned sharply to follow, kicking up rock and sod in a rooster tail and tearing donut shaped furrows into the ground. Then the truck was gaining on her again, and she risked a glance back. In the cab, Ben glared at her hatefully as he and Miles bounced around in their seatbelts on the rough road.

Just then Redwing did something he had never done to Lily before. He bucked her off, and she rolled down the hillside into a stand of scrub oak. Then she heard a terrible thud and the crashing of glass and rending metal, going on and on and on.

She extricated herself painfully from the oak brush and dusted herself off as she walked warily back up to the two-track and followed it back down toward the switchback. Then she heard the quiet whinnying, and she ran to the edge, looking down.

There, just below the corner of the switchback lay Redwing, one leg terribly askew, and she saw that the side of his ribcage was flattened. Still he whinnied as he looked up at her with his wide, soft, eyes, and she ran to him, sobbing.

"Oh Redwing!" she cried, "You saved me again." She knelt at his head, and cradled it in her arms crying and nuzzling his soft nose. He snorted again, spewing a spatter of blood across her new western clothes and cheek, and his barrel chest rose and fell one last time as he died in her arms.

She sat there in the oak brush with Redwing for an interminable time, unable to even consider her next course of action, when she heard shouting from below. She peeked through the oak brush, and saw that an old blue pickup was parked at the ranch house, and a man was running up the slope toward the wrecked red Dodge, which lay upside down at the bottom of a ravine.

"I hope Miles is OK." she thought to herself, though she knew in her heart he was not. Still, the truck had roll bars, so it was possible he lived. Even so, she knew that police and medical personnel were likely on the way, so she walked back to the road on the other side of the house from the driveway, following Reeder Mesa Road back toward the Highway.

"I'm sorry, Miles." she thought. "I am sorry I ever got you into this mess." The tears came again as she considered the cost of her escape. "Redwing… Miles… Sarah… I am so sorry."

She had walked less than a mile when she heard the sirens from Kannah Creek Road. The sirens came again half an hour later, with the sounds travelling the other way. An hour and a half later, she reached Highway 50, turned to the west, and lifted her thumb towards the vehicles traveling back toward Grand Junction.

She wiped away the last of her tears as an I-Roc Camaro pulled over ahead and she ran to catch a ride. The long-haired, forty-something driver smiled at her when she reached the passenger door.

"Hop in!" he said as he reached across the seat and popped open the door. "I'm Ray, where you headed?"

She pulled off her heavy pack and sat down, stowing the pack on the floorboards between her feet. "Hi Ray, I'm Sally." She eased back in the seat and secured her safety belt as he pulled back out onto the highway. "I'm on my way back to California."

"I'm only going to Grand Junction," he said, "kinda out by the mall." He looked over at her a little too appreciatively, continuing, "I've got band rehearsal tonight after I get some chow. You're welcome to hang out."

She realized then how hungry she was. It was late in the afternoon, and she had had nothing but the breakfast sandwich, coffee, and water that day. "I could sure go for something to eat," she said, "but I've got no cash."

He glanced over at her somewhat sharply, so she added, "If you can take me by a pawn shop, I've got some stuff I need to sell anyway."

He looked her over again, and said, "Nah, I got you covered for supper, long as you don't mind Taco Bell." He smiled again, "Wanna hang out at band rehearsal?"

"Sure!" she said, "Sounds like fun!"

She felt better after eating three tacos and downing 32 ounces of Mountain Dew, but she could not remember the names of the other three band members after Ray introduced them. Rehearsal was held in a garage behind a renovated farmhouse not far from the mall, and she sat on an old barstool as the band chatted, tuned, and warmed up.

The band was decent, though their style of heavy metal was not to her tastes. They drank heavily and smoked several joints, and the music deteriorated as the evening wore on. At a break, Ray asked, "Hey Sally, you sing or play any instruments?"

Lily gulped and considered her answer, saying, "Well, I've always loved to sing."

"Cool!" said Ray, "What songs do you know?"

"I can sing along with most anything on the radio," answered Lily, "once I've heard it a few times."

"*Halestorm* did a really cool version of "Still of the Night" by *Whitesnake*." said Ray wryly, "Jamie can't sing it for shit, but maybe you've heard it a few times."

"Fuck you, Ray!" yelled Jamie from the bathroom to laughter from the others.

Lily said, "Maybe I can give it a try, if you aren't too drunk to play it." The laughter continued, and she asked, "Got the lyrics?"

Ray pulled out his phone and said, "I've got it right here on my phone." He fidgeted with the phone for an uncomfortably long time before handing it to Lily and picking up his guitar.

They managed to play a passable version of the song despite their drunkenness, and Lily belted out the lyrics impressively. At the end they all cheered and toasted with beers.

"Yeah!" said Ray, "That fuckin' rocked! "Maybe you can come jam with us again."

Lily smiled and said, "Thanks, man! That was really fun, but I'm on my way to California tomorrow."

The guys all commented that that was too bad, and they smoked another bowl. Lily again declined.

At last, the rehearsal ended and she followed Ray out to his car.

"You got someplace to go tonight?" he asked with a wry grin.

"Not really," she said. "I would get a hotel, but I never made it to the pawn shop for cash."

"You can crash at my place." he said. "You're more than welcome to share my bed, but I got a couch you can use if you want."

"The couch will be fine, thanks." she replied quietly.

He saw her expression change, and added, "Hey, no pressure, Ok?"

She smiled gently, repeating, "No pressure."

"No problem." he said.

"No problem." she repeated.

The next morning, she awoke at dawn, showered quickly, and slipped out the door before he emerged from the bedroom. She walked along the sidewalk toward downtown, pondering her next move. A shop on her way bore a sign reading AAA Pawn and Loan, so she walked in and headed to the counter.

A shaggy, dark haired twenty-something man behind the counter said, "What can I do for you?"

"I have some stuff I'd like to sell for some cash." she said.

"Right on," he replied, "what have you got."

She hefted the heavy pack onto the counter and opened it carefully so that he could not see inside as she withdrew a few pieces of heavy gold jewelry.

He looked at the pieces skeptically at first, but his eyes widened a bit as she handed the items to him and he hefted them. He turned the items over in his hands, examining them carefully.

"where did you get these?" he asked.

"My Grandfather's estate." replied Lily, "He was a collector before he passed on."

"It must have been quite the collection," he noted, "these seem to be genuine historic artifacts."

He looked back at her, and something about his expression worried her, "Do you mind if I call in someone to help me evaluate this stuff?" he asked.

"No," she said, "that's alright, I just need some cash to tide me over for a while."

"No problem," he said, "though I might be able to give you more for them if you're willing to wait for me to talk to my consultant.

"That's OK," she said, "I'll take what I can get for it. What kind of money are we talking about?"

He said, "I can give you $300 for these items right now." He pulled a clipboard of forms from a shelf below the counter. "Just fill out this form and we'll get you the cash."

She smiled and took the clipboard and pen, scanning through the document. She filled in the blank for name as Sally Myers, and made up an address: 1465 Lakeview Drive, Delta, CO, but left the zip code blank. Then she saw the entry for fingerprints, driver's license, and signature attesting to ownership, and she set down the pen.

From under the counter the clerk produced an ink pad and box of tissue, and he glanced at the forms. "You've got to fill out the form completely," he said, "including the zip code and driver's license."

"I don't have a driver's license." she said.

"That's OK," he replied, "just write NA in the box. When you're done with that, I'll just get your fingerprint, and that'll be it."

"You know," she said, "I forgot the zip code for Delta. Have you got a phone book I can use?"

"You bet," he said, turning and walking toward the desk behind the counter.

By the time he turned back around, Lily had snatched up the form from the clipboard, grabbed the jewelry off the counter, and darted out the door to the clanging of the entry bell.

Starving and scared, she ran to the downtown business loop road headed west as she thumbed for a ride. Within minutes a big, white oilfield service truck pulled over, and she jumped in the passenger seat.

The short-haired, heavy-set, muscular, forty something man behind the wheel pulled back out onto the business loop and accelerated with a diesel rattling before he asked, "Where are you headed?"

"California." she said.

Chapter 21: The Way to Freedom

The service truck driver gave her a ride all the way to Las Vegas, after getting food for them at the McDonald's drive through on the way out of town. Daryl, the driver intended to spend his earnings from the oilfield on the good times he was sure to find in the City of Sin. At first, he was a little bit flirtatious with her, but as they chatted he began to realize how young she really was.

Then he talked about his daughter and her progress in school, as well as his aspirations for his daughter's college education. She listened attentively, but the conversation with the doting father made her feel sad as she saw what she would never have again. For the rest of the way, the trip was quiet.

Darkness fell, and she thrilled just a little as the bright lights of the city came into view from the hills east of town. As the city grew closer, Daryl grew more excited.

"I'm staying at the Bellagio," he said, right off the strip.

"Oh," she replied, "is it really nice?"

"Best deal in Vegas," he said, "and really good food."

At the mention of food, her stomach grumbled again, and she was afraid he had heard it when he asked, "Are you OK? Do you need a little money to get you through?"

"Thanks again for breakfast," she said, "you've been far too kind already."

"Hey," he said, "no problem, Kid." He glanced over at her, clearly reading her expression, "Seriously, I can help you out with a little money. I bet your Daddy is worried sick about you. You're too young to be on the streets of Vegas all alone."

"No!" she said as she fought back her tears. Her eyes shined wetly as she added, "My parents are dead, and I have no place safe to go. It's not even safe for you to be around me."

He looked back at her with a hard jaw and said, "If anyone messes with you while I'm around, they're gonna be in a world of hurt." Then his jaw softened and he said, "Hey, just let me treat you to dinner and make sure you've got a safe place for tonight, then we'll see about finding someplace safe for you to live."

They parked in the parking garage at the Bellagio, and made their way to the luxurious lobby, where Daryl picked up the room key card. They made their way to the elevator, and when the doors shut and they felt the vertigo of motion he said, "Bet you've never stayed anywhere as nice as this, huh?"

"No," she said, "this place is amazing."

"The food is even better." he said. "We'll clean up and get settled into the room, then go get some supper."

She looked up at him thankfully. "Sounds great to me!", she said.

Indeed, the food proved to be every bit as delicious as he had said, and she was bleary-eyed and tired by the time they made their way back to the room, which was equipped with two queen-sized beds, a shower and oversized bath, a desk, courtesy bar, and huge flat-screened TV.

He tossed her the TV remote and went to the bathroom, where he urinated loudly, washed up and brushed his teeth before coming back out.

"I'm going out on the town." he said. "Don't wait up." He looked around the room and tapped at his pockets to ensure that he had everything he needed. "No pay per view," he said, "especially not porn, and no drinking from the mini-bar either."

She laughed and nodded agreement, "Of course not!"

Then he went out the door, saying, "See you later, Sally. Stay out of trouble."

"You too," she said, "don't have too much fun."

"Too much is never enough!" he said with a laugh before shutting the door and leaving her alone in the spacious luxury of the Bellagio, Las Vegas.

She worried that somehow, he knew who she was and was alerting the authorities the moment he left, but she slowly relaxed as time wore on. She clicked on the TV and watched the news as it rambled on about a storm and liquor-store robbery.

She fell asleep in bed, sitting against a stack of pillows as the news continued, "There has been a further development in a lead on a quadruple murder investigation in Colorado. The gun used in the murders was discovered in the vehicle of the son of murder victim Jake Vigil after an accident."

"The son, Mr. Benjamin Vigil, died in the suspicious one-vehicle accident on Tuesday, which also critically injured museum curator Miles Dunbury. The accident remains under investigation, and Mr. Dunbury remains in critical condition. Authorities are still seeking Miss DuCray, who is also considered armed and dangerous. Anyone having information regarding this case or any other serious crime is asked to call 1-800-222-TIPS."

Lily awoke when Daryl came in. He tried to be quiet, but she could hear his heavy breath and uneven footsteps, and the fan came on when he stepped into the bathroom and urinated noisily.

She pretended to be asleep as he returned to the room and whispered, "G'nite, Sally." He kissed her lightly on the cheek, adding, "Sleep well." before crawling into his own bed.

She slept like a stone until morning.

Daryl woke early, and the sound of the shower woke her. She dressed quickly, just in case, and clicked on the TV while she waited for him to finish.

"Did ya have fun?" she asked when he re-appeared clad in a towel.

"I'm sure I must have." he replied, "How about you."

"Slept like a rock." she said. "Thanks again for everything you've done for me. I don't know what I would have done without your help."

"No problem," he said, "how about some breakfast?"

"Sounds great," she said, "I hoped you would ask."

At breakfast, the short, dark haired waitress was efficient, but the way she looked at Daryl was accusatory. To Lily she was sweet, but almost condescending as she brought out their coffee and juice. Her name tag read 'Glenda'

At first, she was puzzled by the waitress' reaction, until Daryl said, "She thinks I am taking advantage of you."

"If anyone is taking advantage, it's me." said Lily. "You've been a perfect gentleman. How would she know I'm not just your daughter?"

"Men my age don't generally bring daughters your age to Vegas." he said. "What she thinks is going on is much more common, I suppose." He took a sip of his coffee, and added, "No worries, we're not criminals."

The waitress returned silently with their plates: bacon and eggs over-medium for him, pancakes, eggs, and sausage for her.

She sipped her own coffee and tried not to look worried, as he asked, "Where are you headed in Cali?"

She swallowed the coffee and said, "L.A., I think. But, maybe San Diego, I really like it there."

"What's in California to make you want to go there so bad." he asked.

"I dunno," she admitted. "I really don't know anyone there anymore. Just good memories." She hung her head a little and picked at a pancake with her fork. "Just memories of my Dad and Mom before…"

"I'm sorry to bring it up." he said, "You obviously know what you're running from, but you need to think about where you're running to, also."

She took a bite of the delicious light, fluffy pancake, but the flavor turned to ash in her mouth. "You're right." she mumbled.

"I usually am." he said. "Here is two hundred dollars. Use it to get someplace safe." He slid the money across the table to her, and Lily saw the waitress' eyes narrow as she traded out coffee pots at the busing station.

Lily opened her pack, which she had brought down with her. Then she pulled out a necklace of gold and Jade, which she slid across the table to him. "Give this to your daughter, and remind her how lucky she is to have you as her father."

She stood up suddenly and gave him a peck on the cheek. "Thanks for everything!" she said, "You are truly wonderful."

Then she turned her heel and walked as fast as she could toward the lobby. As she turned the corner, she saw the waitress talking to two hotel security officers, but they did not notice her and she darted through the lobby and out the rotating glass doors.

She hurried through the valet area to the sidewalk along Lake Bellagio to the Strip itself, Las Vegas Boulevard, trying to disappear in the thin crowds. At the information kiosk, she searched for the bus depot on the map, and sat down to wait for a local route bus to come by.

Then the two hotel security officers from the Bellagio came out the rotating doors, looking her way down the sidewalk. One of the security officers thumbed the button of the lapel microphone wired to his radio as they hustled along towards her.

She jumped to her feet and ran, darting across the street at the red light just before it turned green and the stream of vehicles resumed. The security officers stopped at the kiosk, trying to keep an eye on her through the traffic.

At the entrance to the Paris Las Vegas she turned, hurrying toward the massive building then reversing to hide behind and follow a bus back to the strip. She doubled back to the south, making her way along the Strip and turning onto the sidewalk of Harmon Street toward the bus depot.

Glancing back, she saw a police car rolling slowly down the Paris access Road.

It took a bit over an hour to walk to the bus depot, and she stood in the short line for a ticket, just watching her fellow travelers. Next to the line was a plastic sandwich board reading, "If you see something, say something. Crime stops with you."

Several televisions hung from brackets in the corners of the room though she could not hear any sound from the broadcasts. She glanced at one of the screens just in time to see her own picture appear on an inset above the pretty newswoman with a 1-800 phone number.

Her heart raced, and the sweat of her long walk in the desert heat turned suddenly clammy. She glanced around to see if anyone was looking at her strangely, and only then noticed that she had come to the front of the line and the attendant was talking to her.

"…travelling today?" was all she heard.

"Um, yes," she said, "I'd like a ticket to Las Angeles, please."

"Ok, Miss," replied the dark-haired twenty-something attendant, "Do you have any baggage?"

"Just my back pack." she replied.

"Would you like to check it, or carry it with you?" he inquired.

"I'd like to keep it with me." she replied.

"No problem, Miss." he said, "We have a departure scheduled for 1pm this afternoon. If I can just see a photo ID and forty-eight dollars."

Lily's face flushed red, and she stammered a bit before saying, "I'm sorry, I don't have a driver's license or anything like that."

The attendant gave her a fake, sad frown and said, "I'm sorry, Miss, I can't sell you a ticket without a valid photo ID."

She looked scared for a moment, unsure whether to ask more questions or flee, so he added, "You can obtain photo ID at any DMV or Social Services office for a nominal fee."

"Um," she said as she turned and began to hurry away, "thanks."

She glanced back at the desk before allowing the door to close behind her. The woman who had been standing behind her in line was showing the attendant something on her phone screen, and both turned to look at her at the door.

She let go of the door and ran. At the sidewalk, she headed south along Decatur Street. There were many little retail and office shops scattered along the road. She passed Mexican, German, and Mediterranean restaurants where the lunchtime food was being prepared, and she realized she was hungry again.

She opted for the busiest of her options, called 'The Hacienda', darting inside with a glance back up the road toward the bus depot. She was seated by the pretty, but disinterested hostess at a booth for two along the back wall.

She ordered a green chili chicken burrito, a Coke, and water when the Mexican waiter brought her chips and salsa. Then she chomped some chips and salsa and tried to calm down. Her food arrived quickly, and she ate as much of the oversized burrito as she could before paying and going back out into the heat.

The walking and running she had done and the big meal she had eaten left her lethargic, and she plodded to the corner, following the signs for I-15 down West Sunset Road, where she could soon see the Interstate overpass ahead.

At the entrance ramp, she darted back behind a tour bus as she saw a police cruiser slowly trolling along, the passenger-side officer plainly scanning the ramp area for someone.

When the cruiser had passed, she trotted up the entry ramp until she could clearly see the sign forbidding pedestrians beyond that point. Then she waited and stuck out her thumb at every vehicle that passed.

This time it was a beat up older VW Jeta that pulled to the side. A big, black Labrador in the back seat wagged its tail and hopped up on the backrest of the seat to look out the back window at her as she ran up to the passenger door.

As she opened the door, the tall, skinny, long-haired blonde in a purple hippy dress behind the wheel said, "You can put your pack on the floorboards in the back. Bruno won't mess with it."

She mumbled, "Thanks." as she got in and put on her seat belt.

"Where are you headed?" asked the blonde as she guided the jalopy back onto the ramp and accelerated onto I-15 West.

"L.A." said Lily, "how about you?"

"Yeah, me too." said the driver. "I got a ticket to see Imagine Dragons tonight at the Staples Center"

"Wow!" exclaimed Lily, "that sounds awesome!"

"Yeah," the girl responded, "it is gonna be awesome. A whole group of us girlfriends are going. I can hardly wait."

"Sounds really cool!" added Lily. "How much are tickets?"

"I think it was a hundred and ten bucks or so," she replied, "but it'll be worth it."

"where are you staying in L.A.?" the girl asked.

"I dunno yet," replied Lily, "I don't really know anyone there, but I'll figure something out."

"They might still have tickets," the girl said, "if you've got the money."

"I have a little bit," Lily replied, "but I probably should save it just in case."

"Just in case of what?" asked the blonde playfully.

"Um," stammered Lily, "I dunno. I've got some stuff I need to sell, but I don't know how easy it will be." She looked down at her lap for a moment, and added, "Until then, all I've got is a hundred and eighty bucks."

"That doesn't get you very far in L.A." said the girl. "just a couple of nights at a cheap hotel." She looked over at Lily, saying, "Cowgirl, huh?"

"Kinda," said Lily, "but my horse is dead, and I had to run away from the ranch."

The driver gave Lily a look of genuine sympathy. "I'm really sorry to hear that." she said. "Every girl loves horses. I never got to have one, but I bet it's really sad when your horse dies."

Lily nodded, but did not look up.

The driver concentrated on the road for a moment, then looked back to Lily and extended her hand. "I'm Marsha Taylor," she said, glad to meet you..."

"Lil...", she began, "Sally Myers."

Marsha laughed and said, "I've heard of Lil Wayne, and Lil Kim, and now Lil Sally Myers."

Lily reddened with embarrassment, and Marsha added, "I'm sorry, I didn't mean to make fun of you, it was just cute is all."

At that point the Bruno could bear being ignored in the back seat no longer. He placed his big forepaws on the center console and gave Lily a big wet lick on the cheek, which set both girls laughing. Lily patted and ruffled his head for a moment, and his tail thump thumped against the back of Marsha's seat and the back seat for a few minutes. Satisfied with the attention, he turned around three times on the seat and lay back down.

After some time of silence, Marsha asked, "So how old are you, Sally?"

"Eighteen," said Lily a bit too quickly.

"OK," replied Marsha unconvincingly, continuing, "L.A. is a terrible place to run away to." She looked back at Lily and saw the fear in her eyes. "That town will eat you up if you're not careful."

Lily looked down again, worried.

"The concert might be a great place to get rid of whatever you're selling out of that backpack, though." said Marsha, "but watch out for the undercover cops. A lotta people get busted selling drugs at shows."

Lily started and exclaimed, "I don't have any drugs!"

"Yeah?" said Marsha, "What else is sold out of backpacks by runaways?"

"It's antiques," said Lily defensively, "old jewelry and stuff. You know, worth a lot, but only to the right people."

"Oh," said Marsha with a sideways smile, "I was kinda hoping you had some good shit."

Lily chuckled anxiously and shook her head.

"Listen," said Marsha, "I've got a place you could stay, just for a few days until you get your shit together. My roommate Amie just moved out. It's not much, but it's way better than being on the street. I might even be able to find you a job, if you don't mind working."

"I'm a good worker." said Lily, "but I don't have any ID, so it makes it really hard."

"Hell, half the workforce of California probably doesn't have a valid ID." said Marsha, "Just refuse to answer any questions and they can't do anything to you unless they actually catch you in a crime. L.A. is the fake ID capitol of the world. I'm sure we can find you one."

"OK." said Lily, "I'd really like to go to the concert tonight."

Marsha smiled widely. "It's on, then!" she said, "We're gonna have a great time!"

Chapter 22: No Dirt Nap

The girls really did have a great time at the concert, and they stopped for a late night meal afterwards, chatting like old friends. She had never been to a big concert before, and she loved every second of the loud music and bright lights. Though the big crowds were intimidating, they made it easy for her to feel anonymous and safe from pursuit.

She had borrowed a cute tan skirt and white blouse from Marsha with assurances that they would be returned undamaged or replaced. She still wore her beat-up old boots.

Until that night, she had only drunk alcohol on a few occasions, and had never tried any illegal drugs. But that night she and the girls drank several bottles of wine and smoked a few joints before going out. Once at the concert, she refused the LSD blotter square offered to her by Marsha's friend Amie, but the whole experience still seemed psychedelic.

After the concert, Amie and a little brunette named Katie invited them to an after-party at the apartment of a sometimes boyfriend of Katie. Marsha was reluctant to attend, but she saw the curiosity and excitement in Lily's eyes, and they found themselves arriving at the apartment at 2:45 am.

Marsha looked over at Lily as they prepared to get out of the vehicle. "Are you sure you're up for this?" asked Marsha, "It's pretty late."

Lily looked at her with tired excitement, "I'm game if you are."

The apartment was on the fourth floor and featured a small balcony overlooking the upscale apartment complex pool. Lily had barely entered the door of the crowded apartment when she decided that she and Marsha should have just gone back to Marsha's place and gone to bed.

The place was packed with fashionably dressed twenty-somethings, and she felt the familiar anxiety she had acquired at her cliquish high school. The other party-goers largely ignored them except for a few glances, and they looked for Marsha's friends in the crowd.

They found Amie and Katie on the balcony in boisterous conversation with a few young men. "Come on," said the shortest of the men with a grin, "you take it all off at the club, you can show us a little something, too."

"Yeah," said Katie, "but we get paid to take it off at the club."

"Hey," the short dark-haired man said, "this will be a lot more fun than the club." He leaned over the even smaller Katie with a hand on the tan stucco wall, "They don't allow booze at the club, and we got some good coke, too."

"Oh yeah?" said Katie flirtatiously, "Who's gonna protect us if you naughty boys get all touchy-feely?"

Then Amie interrupted, "Oh, hey guys, this is my friends Marsha and... Sally."

Marsha and Lily gave a little wave and said "Hi, guys."

Amie gestured toward the three men in turn, saying, "this is Leo, David, and Martin."

"Hey Ladies," said Leo, David, and Martin with smiles as they extended hands to Marsha and Lily in turn.

"Welcome to the party!" said Martin as he turned and put his arm around Katie's small waist. "We were just about to go into the back room to have some coke and a smile."

"Yeah!" said Katie, "We'll show you how to party L.A. style."

"Marsha and Lily respectively said, "No thanks, I can't stay long." and "Sure, sounds fun!" at the same time. The whole group laughed, and Martin began leading them into the apartment, through the kitchen and dining area down the hall to a closed bedroom. He opened the door and the seven of them filed in.

The bedroom décor was modern, with chrome accented dark grey furniture and red and gray drapes, pillowcases and bedding.

Martin sat on the bed with Katie close beside him, and he opened the nightstand drawer, pulling out a small mirror, straw, and prescription bottle. He then proceeded to lay out a series of powder lines on the mirror from the prescription bottle while the others found places to sit on the bed, floor, and dresser top.

Lily sat on the end of the bed, and Leo sat down next to her. He wore tan dockers and a form-fitting red golf shirt, and his muscular, bare arm sent a thrill through her as it touched her skin.

Martin sniffed up the first line, then leaned back with watery eyes. "Ladies first," he said, gesturing to Katie toward the mirror. Katie leaned sensuously over Martin's lap, took up the straw, and sniffed up the second line, pausing to kiss Martin passionately before sitting up.

"Your turn," said Katie to Lily with a shiny-eyed grin.

Lily rose, then knelt before the nightstand in front of Katie and Martin. Then she picked up the straw and glanced around the room again. Marsha leaned against the dresser, watching Lily carefully. Amie and David sat on the other side of the bed, making out. Martin and Katie looked at Lily almost hungrily.

"Go for it!" said Katie, "Let's get this party started."

At that, Lily leaned over the mirror, trying to sniff up the coke as she had seen Leo and Katie do. Instead, she sniffed hard and the coke burned in her sinuses and throat, causing her to snort convulsively. The remaining lines sprayed across the nightstand and she fell back on her heels to rub her watering eyes.

"Party foul!" said Amie as she came up for air, "Looks like we got us a cocaine virgin."

"Sorry!" stammered Lily. "I've never done anything like this before."

Martin glared at her, but Katie said, "It's OK, girl, we got more."

Lily rose again and returned to her seat on the end of the bed as Martin laid out more lines and Amie moved to take her place in front of the nightstand. Lily's head began buzzing, and she felt tingly all over. She hardly noticed Leo put his arm around her, and she did not resist when he placed a hand behind her head and gave her a passionate kiss.

She tingled even more, and could feel her blood racing through her veins as Leo placed a hand on her thigh. Embroiled in the kiss, she did not see Marsha leave the room, and she merely quivered with excitement when Leo slid his hands up below her skirt to the moistness of her swollen mons.

His moistened fingers then began probing into her, spreading her lips and driving in to rub against her from inside. She moaned in oblivion as he worked her with fingers, finally sliding to his knees at the foot of the bed and hiking her skirt above her waist. His tongue and lips replaced his fingers, and he licked and sucked her clit and stuffed his tongue into her hole.

Then, when she felt the building pressure of orgasm approaching, he stood and plunged his engorged cock into her suddenly. The world seemed to explode outward from her pussy, and she screamed with pain and ecstasy. She convulsed several more times as he pounded into her, slapping his balls against her ass with her legs wrapped around his waist.

Then he hunched up, gritting his teeth and grunting before rearing back with a roar. His hot seed erupted into her as his cock surged and spat. He stroked into her a few more times, and she felt the wetness run down between her ass cheeks over her butthole as he pulled out his still rampant cock.

He smiled down at her, saying, "Wow, that was hot!" Then he noticed the blood and asked, "Are you starting your period?"

"No," she said meekly, and his eyes widened a bit.

"Wow," he exclaimed, "you were a virgin."

She nodded quietly, self-conscious now that the passion was sated and the coke wearing off. She noticed the others still in the room. Amie and David still fucked slowly on the floor beside the bed, though all she could see was David's churning back and ass between Amie's knees. Katie knelt in front of Martin on the other side of the bed, repeatedly taking his shaft deep into her tiny throat.

She gulped, suddenly thirsty, embarrassed, and sore. Leo stepped back from the bed and reached for his pants and underwear, which he quickly stepped into. Lily closed her legs and re-settled her skirt, looking for her underwear on the floor as Leo sat down next to her.

He slipped on his socks and loafers, looking over at her with some consternation. "You Ok?" he asked.

She nodded, her dry throat constricted. She snatched up her embarrassingly juvenile underwear and started to slip them on, but felt her pussy leaking cum. Then she gave Leo a wan smile and rose, quickly opening the door and exiting to shut it behind her. Down the hall, the bathroom door was closed, so she leaned against the wall and waited.

Leo came out of the bedroom a moment later, and he gave her a kiss before continuing out to the kitchen. When at last the bathroom door opened, two other girls came out, both bleary eyed and clumsy. They each looked at Lily and laughed, then headed to the kitchen as well.

Lily hurried to the pot, sat, and released the cum and a long stream of tinkling urine with a sigh. When she finished, she carefully wiped up the mess and washed her hands, face and privates with a washcloth she found in the cabinet below the sink. Finally, she looked in the mirror and shook her head.

By the time she got back to the kitchen, the party was dying fast. Most of the guests had gone, and she looked around desperately for Marsha. The balcony was empty, and someone had fallen asleep on the couch. Beer bottles and disposable cups covered nearly every surface, and Leo, too, had apparently gone.

She was in a near panic when Amie reappeared from the hall. "That was one hell of a party!" she said, looking around. "You sure are a hot mess. I still can't believe you were a virgin."

"Yeah," said Lily flatly, "I'm definitely fucked all right."

Amie looked back at her again with a touch of concern in her jaded eyes.

"I've been figuratively fucked for a long time," said Lily, "but now I am really fucked." She looked back at Amie and added, "I was supposed to stay at Marsha's, but she left when I started acting like an idiot." She started to cry, blinking and wiping the tears with the back of her fists. "Leo just left when I went to the bathroom. I thought he really liked me."

"He was sure liking you plenty back in Martin's room," said Amie, "and it sure sounded like you were having fun." Amie put her arm around Lily's shoulders and continued, "Come on, girl, we got to live a little before we take a dirt nap."

Lily snorted, but smiled through the tears. "Yeah, it was a really fun night. I'm just really tired and worried that I ruined it with Marsha. She's been so nice to me, I feel like a jerk for ditching her for Leo."

"You didn't ditch her," said Amie, "she just bailed on you once you started having fun. You can stay with me tonight, Katie is spending the night with Martin."

"What about David?" asked Lily.

"David's all right," replied Amie, "but he's not really 'spend the night' material." She grinned at Lily sassily, "Sometimes a girl just wants to have fun. Let's get out of here."

They laughed as they ran out through the chilly pre-dawn air to Amie's Nissan Altima and raced through the back streets to Amie's less impressive apartment. There was little chatter as they both just wanted to sleep. Amie tossed some blankets and a pillow onto the couch, poured herself a glass of water from the tap, and disappeared into her bedroom.

Within minutes, Lily was asleep.

Lily awoke as Katie came in looking much more ragged than she had the night before, "Good morning, sunshine!" she said unconvincingly as Lily opened her eyes from the couch. "What a night!" She rustled around the kitchen for a few minutes and announced, "Off to bed, gotta work late tonight."

Lily could not sleep any more, and she got up and went to the kitchen, found the coffee, and brewed up a cup with the Keurig. Then she sat on the couch to think. Amie came in shortly after, making herself a cup and joining Lily in the living room.

"How'd ya sleep?" she asked.

"Not too bad." replied Lily. "Thanks for letting me stay."

"No problem," replied Amie, "happy to help a sister out."

"I need to get a fake ID," said Lily, "so I can get a job and pawn some things."

"Getting a fake ID shouldn't be too hard," said Amie, "I know some people who can help with that. As hot as you are, I'm sure I can get you a job at the club. They always want new talent. Can you dance?"

Lily sat silent for a moment, then said, "Kinda, I mean I've never really tried to dance like that."

"You'll learn," said Amie, "we can teach you. It's really good money, and sometimes it's pretty fun, too."

"I'm almost out of money now," said Lily, "but I've got some really valuable antiques I can sell if I can find the right buyer."

"What kind of valuable antiques have you got?" asked Amie.

"Some Aztec treasure, I think." replied Lily, "Probably have to go black market."

"Really?" asked Amie, "where'd you find that stuff?"

"I found it," replied Lily, "but I can't tell anyone where."

"Oooh," said Amie, "A hot young chick with hot merchandise. Sounds exciting."

"It was exciting," said Lily, "way too exciting."

Amie nodded but asked no more questions. "When we get cleaned up, we'll go see Hector the Fence, down at the Paycheck loan place. He's a regular at the club, and he's got connections in the Mexican Mafia." Amie saw Lily's expression of concern, and added, "He's a nice guy, though, and he always has good coke."

"I'm not sure I want to try that again." said Lily.

Amie just smiled her jaded smile.

Lily got her fake California Motor Vehicle License later that day from Hector at the Payday Loan. Hector was very charming, and told the girls he would see them at the club that night. Lily asked Hector if he could help her find a buyer for some Aztec artifacts, and he was very intrigued, so Lily pulled a few gold and jade items from her pack.

Hector looked over the items with interest, and asked if he might keep one to present to a prospective buyer, and Lily agreed. Hector was still examining the gold torque when the girls left.

"Listen," said Amie when they got back into her car, "you're gonna need some new clothes if you want to work at the club. I saw the way Hector looked at your stuff, and I'm sure you'll have some money in your hot little hands real soon."

"Yeah," said Lily, "I sure hope so."

"Me too," added Amie, "but I was thinking we could go shopping and get whatever you need, and you can pay me back tonight or whenever Hector comes through with a deal."

"That'd be great!" said Lily.

Off they went shopping at the mall, and Lily had rarely felt so much like a normal girl. They laughed and tried on different outfits, buying a few for each of them. Lily also bought a little bit of makeup with Amie's help.

At last Lily threw her old beat up cowboy boots into the trashcan at the mall after buying a nice pair of sneakers and a pair of sexy high heels.

"I don't imagine I'll be riding a horse any time soon." she said to Amie.

"Did you have a horse?" asked Amie.

"Yes," said Lily with shiny eyes, "and he was my best friend."

"Ooh," responded Amie, "did you have to leave him behind wherever you're from?"

"He died," she said with a sad smile, "saving me from an evil man."

"So here you are in Cali," said Amie, "with a brand new bestie!"

"Yeah!" said Lily, "and a brand new life."

"I'll drink to that." said Amie, "Let's pick up a bottle of vodka and some OJ on the way back."

They ate falafel at the Pita Pit and bought the vodka and orange juice at the neighboring grocery, then went back to Amie and Katie's apartment.

There they found Katie already dressed for the club. She wore thigh high red faux leather heels and a matching mini-dress, and was packing her other club costumes into her black duffle bag. Then Amie went to shower and get dressed, leaving Lily to chat with Katie.

"So where are you from, Sally?" asked Katie as she put on her makeup.

"I'm originally from San Diego." replied Lily as she sat at the kitchen table.

"Oh," responded Katie, "it's really nice there. Where are you staying here in L.A.?"

"Well I was gonna stay at Marsha's," said Lily, "but then she kinda ditched me while we were all fooling around at Martin's party. I sure didn't mean to piss her off."

"I don't think Marsha likes sexy parties or strip clubs." said Katie. "That's why Amie moved in with me."

"Oh." said Lily sadly, "Maybe I should have gone back with her instead of getting with Leo."

"Maybe so," said Katie, "I dunno. Depends on what you're into."

"I guess I don't know what I'm into yet." said Lily.

"Maybe you'll find out tonight." said Katie. "Either way, you're gonna have to find someplace else to stay." Katie said, "Martin is out of town and I am working tonight, so we can't really have any couch crashers."

"Oh," said Lily, "I was hoping to come to the club tonight to talk to Hector and see about getting a job." There was a momentary silence, and she continued, "Maybe Amie can drop me off at Marsha's on the way back from the club."

"Marsha may not be too excited to see you after the party," said Katie as she hefted her bag and headed to the door. "Maybe you better call her."

Lily did call her, borrowing Amie's phone when she got out of the shower.

"Hi Marsha," said Lily after Marsha picked up, "it's Sally."

"Oh," responded Marsha, "How are you doing?"

"Great!" responded Lily a bit too enthusiastically, "how about you."

"I'm fine." said Marsha, "How did the rest of the party go? It looked like you were having too much fun."

"Yeah," Lily said, "maybe so." There was a pause, and she continued, "I was kinda hoping I could still be your roommate, if you're not too pissed at me."

"I'm not pissed at you, Sally," said Marsha, "just worried for you. You're gonna get into real trouble hanging out with Martin and Leo and that bunch at the club. They are involved in the Mexican Mafia, and girls like you disappear all the time."

There was silence, as Lily could think of nothing to say, then Marsha said, "Hey, you are welcome to be my roommate. I like you a lot. Just be careful, OK?"

"OK," Lily said. "I'll be careful."

"OK," said Marsha, "then I'll see you in the wee hours of the morning. Just call me when you get here or if you need to get out of there."

"OK," Lily replied, "thank you so much."

"You're welcome so much." said Marsha, "Bye."

"Bye!" said Lily.

She hung up the phone, relieved to have a friend and a place to stay. Then she hurried to shower and get ready for the night at the club. By the time she got out of the shower, Amie was already dressed in a tight zebra print slit skirt dress and was putting on makeup.

Lily put on her new, black mini-dress and began to apply her makeup, when Amie walked by. Amie saw Lily struggling with her technique, and chuckled, "What are you doing it that way for?"

Lily paused, looked over at Amie and said, "What do you mean?"

Amie looked aghast as she said, "Have you never put on makeup before?"

Lily looked chagrined, and answered, "Just a couple of times. I never had any makeup before."

"You poor thing!" said Amie, "Let me help you out with that. Then we gotta get going."

Amie helped Lily apply her makeup, stepped back and said, "Yeah! Now we look super-hot. Let's go!"

They arrived at the Fantasy Girls Gentleman's club half an hour before Amie was scheduled to dance. Amie introduced Lily to the doorman, a burly bald guy with no neck called Webb. Amie then took Lily back to the green room, where the ladies prepared for their dances.

Katie was already on the floor, doing a pole dance and hanging upside down. Already a half-dozen men sat along what Amie called the chow line around the "H" shaped catwalk and stage.

"There are two kinds of strip clubs in California," said Amie, "the kind where they serve booze, but the ladies wear panties, and the kind where they don't serve alcohol, but the ladies get completely naked."

Lily listened wide-eyed, and nodded, "Uh-huh."

Amie smiled, "At Fantasy Girls, we get naked."

"Oh," said Lily again.

"Either way," continued Amie, "there are rules. The patrons are not allowed to touch us, but we can touch them if we want. No open sex, but we want to keep them excited. We get paid minimum wage," continued Amie, "but we get tips, and the good dancers make good money, at least a couple hundred a night."

"Sometimes the guys want a private dance, and that's twenty bucks right off the bat, plus tips." Amie looked squarely at Lily, "We aren't prostitutes, but sometimes guys will offer a lot of money for actual sex in the private rooms. You've gotta make sure you know your customer if you take them up on that, 'cause the cops do stings every once in a while, and that's usually how they catch people."

Lily looked almost terrified, and didn't say a word.

"Listen," said Amie, "I know this is a lot to take in, especially for someone who was a virgin yesterday, but I think you'll have a great time once you learn the ropes."

Lily nodded uncertainly.

Anyway," said Amie, "why don't you come out to the floor and watch a few sets." She handed Lily a few dollars cash, "You can give these out as tips, just slip them in the G-string or on the floor. You'll see. You should also go meet Wayne, the DJ. Make sure he gets a cut of the tips, so you get the hype and good choices of music."

"Go ahead on out," said Amie. "I'm on in just a second, but you should see the end of Katie's set. She is really good."

"OK!" said Lily as firmly as she could, "See you out there."

Amie waved with a fake smile, and Lily went back out to the floor, looking more carefully around. The DJ booth sat at the back of the room at the foot of one of the legs of the catwalk 'H', so Lily walked back to the booth and waited for the dark-haired DJ to look up.

When he finished starting the next CD, Lily said, "Hi Wayne, I'm Sally, a friend of Amie and Katie." as she extended her hand.

Wayne looked up at her through thick glasses, and reached over to take her hand gently, "Nice to meet you, Sally. The beginnings of a familiar sounding industrial song began, And Lily watched Katie as she moved her near-naked body in perfect synchronism to the jarring music.

"You bring me closer to God." sang Trent Reznor at the chorus, "I want to fuck you like an animal." Lily's eyes widened unconsciously at the provocative lyrics and sexy dance, "I want to feel you from the inside."

Her pussy tingled a bit, and she walked over to the chow line and sat on a padded chair. Katie sauntered over, kneeling in front of Lily with spread knees and arching her back sensually. Then Katie splayed her legs to the side and rolled backward gracefully to her feet, stepping closer so that lily could slide a bill into her G-string.

Then Katie moved on to entice the men on the chow line. Lily gulped, seeing the men looking at her and Katie so hungrily.

The dance ended, and Wayne announced, "Alright everybody, let's give the Incredible Katie Q a great big hand out there." The growing crowd cheered and clapped for a few moments, and Wayne continued, "Up next we've got Amazing Amie Storm to keep you going strong out there. Don't forget to tip your waitresses and bartender as they're working hard to keep you satisfied."

A Bruno Mars song started on the sound system, and out came Amie, looking sexy as she slid sensually out onto the stage. She slid one foot forward, exposing a great deal of thigh through her slit skirt, and bent forward at the waist to give the best glimpse of her cleavage and ass through the tight skirt.

Katie made her way around the room, chatting and flirting with the men on the chow line as she made herself available for private dances. She said "Hi!" to Lily as she passed, and laid a warm hand on Lily's shoulder for a moment. Then one of the men asked for a dance, so she took his hand and led him back to the private rooms separated from the main room by heavy curtains.

By the third song, Amie was naked, and at least a dozen men sat along the chow line. Lily looked around, having been fixated on Amie's dancing and the sexual atmosphere along the chow line. In came Hector, with a friendly wave to Webb at the door.

He looked around, saw Lily, and made his way over to her, offering his hand as he sat. "Sally," he said, "good to see you again."

"You too, Hector." said Lily.

He settled in and the waitress came over and asked, "What would you like to drink?"

Hector ordered iced tea, and Lily a Coke, then Lily asked, "Did you get a chance to show that piece to your guy?"

Before he could answer, the waitress returned with the drinks. Hector took a sip as he watched Amie dance. "Yes," he said, "I did." Lily sipped her Coke as she waited for him to continue. "I can offer you five hundred for that piece, and my buyer has offered to take any other similar items off your hands for a good price."

"Cool!" said Lily, "but I was hoping to get a little more from that piece. I'm pretty sure it's authentic, and it's definitely real gold."

Hector looked over at her with an implacable expression. "I can give you a grand for it." he said, "and will take as much of that kind of merchandise as you can get." He smiled over at Lily, "Sound good?"

"Sounds great!" she said, "thanks a lot!"

"No problem," said Hector, "always a pleasure doing business with such a beautiful young lady."

He shook her hand again, smiling with bright eyes and a tight grin. Then he reached into his jacket, withdrawing an envelope. "Here you are, one thousand dollars." He slid the envelope to Lily along the wide chow line rail, and asked, "Do you have any more of the artifacts with you."

"Yes," she said, "They're in my pack back in the green room."

"Let me take that off your hands tonight," said Hector, "and I'll get you paid tomorrow after I have a chance to get the merchandise appraised."

"OK," said Lily, "Do you want it now?"

"No," replied Hector, "Just get it for me when Amie goes on break."

"OK," said Lily, "No problem."

They watched the rest of Amie's set, and Amie made her way around the room, sitting to chat with Hector and Lily for just a moment.

"Hey Hector," said Amie, "nice to see you."

"You, too, Amie." said Hector, extending his hand. When she shook his hand, he gently raiser her hand to his lips and kissed it. "Mon Amie," he said.

"Ooh," she said, "getting all exotic on me, are you."

"Of course," said Hector, "exotic and erotic as well."

"You naughty boy," she said. "Are you up for a private dance?"

"Of course!" said Hector, "lead the way."

Hector and Amie retreated behind the curtains, and Lily went back to the green room to get her pack. As she opened the "Employees Only" door, she saw Katie digging through Lily's pack.

Katie looked up as Lily came in, smiling sheepishly.

"What the hell, Katie?" said Lily sharply, "What are you doing digging through my stuff?"

"I just needed to fix my makeup," said Katie defensively, "and I thought I might borrow some fresh lipstick."

"Bullshit!" said Lily, "I have almost nothing, but you were gonna rip me off."

"Come on, Sally!" exclaimed Katie, "I was just curious what you had in there that was so valuable. I wasn't going to take anything."

Lily snatched the pack from Katie, looking through the contents to ensure that nothing was taken.

"I'm sorry, Sally." Katie said, "please don't tell anyone."

"OK, Katie." Lily said. "Just don't steal from me, OK. I want to be your friend."

"OK, Sally," Katie said, "let's be friends."

The two girls hugged, but the tension remained, and Lily retreated to the main room with her pack. When Hector returned from the private room, Lily joined him at a table away from the chow line.

"Well," said Hector, "I think I'm gonna go by Chili's for dinner on my way home." He looked expectantly at Lily, and she handed him the backpack.

"Would you mind if I joined you for dinner?" asked Lily, "Maybe you can drop me off at Marsha's on your way? I'm not sure I'm cut out to work here."

"No problem, Sally." said Hector, "You're welcome to join me, and I'd be happy to drop you off at Marsha's, if you show me where it is."

Dinner was uneventful, and Hector was as charming as could be, though Lily sensed a bit of coldness in his eyes and demeanor. He kissed her hand gently before she got out of his silver Lexus, and asked her to come by the Payday Loan the next day.

Marsha welcomed her in with a little relief when she knocked on the door. "I'm glad you decided not to stay out at the club all night." Marsha said as she gave Lily a genuine hug, "It's not a healthy atmosphere there."

"No," said Lily, "and Katie doesn't really like me. I don't trust her."

"You shouldn't trust her," said Marsha as she brought Lily back to arm's length and looked into her eyes, "she's a bad influence."

"Yeah," said Lily, "and I don't really think stripping is the right job for me. Do you still think you can find me a job?"

"Sure," said Marsha, "I'm pretty sure I can help you get a job. Not as exciting or high-paying as stripping, but a lot easier on the soul."

Marsha let go of Lily's shoulders, heading to the kitchen. "Did you eat yet?" she asked.

"Yeah," Lily said, "I had some Chili's on the way here."

"How'd you get home?" she asked, "Cab?"

"No, I got a ride from Hector." Lily admitted.

Marsha turned back to Lily sharply, saying, "I really wish you hadn't done that. Now he knows where we live."

"Oh," said Lily, "I hadn't thought of that."

Marsha shook her head, "I don't know what I'm gonna do with you," she said, "to keep you out of trouble. I know Hector is charming, and he seems like a nice guy, but those people are really dangerous. You don't even want to know the kind of crime they are up to. Fake IDs and cocaine are just the tip of the iceberg with them."

"I'm sorry, Marsha," said Lily, "I kinda had to deal with him to get the ID and sell my stuff."

"I hope you got what it was worth," said Marsha, "or at least close to it."

"I got a thousand right up front," Lily elaborated, "with a whole lot more coming tomorrow. At least it'll give me a good start here, and I can go get more when the money runs low."

"I sure hope you're right," Marsha cautioned, "but you can't trust those guys, so watch out."

"I will." assured Lily.

"I hope so." said Marsha.

The next day, Lily rode with Marsha to the Payday Loan, where Marsha waited in the car. Hector invited Lily right into his office, where he shook her hand gently and shut the door.

He gestured to the visitor's chair and sat in his office chair before saying, "Good morning, Sally. I take it you had a pleasant evening last night."

"I sure did," she replied, "thanks for everything."

"My pleasure." He said with a charming smile. "Now as for the goods you brought me: My buyer has authorized me to purchase the rest for two hundred thousand dollars."

He looked up squarely into Lily's eyes, clearly reading her shock and excitement. "He has also asked that if you should have a line on more of these artifacts, he would gladly purchase them at a similar rate." She didn't respond at first, so he asked, "What do you think?"

"Sounds great!", she said, "When can I get the first of the money?"

He slid a fat stack of bills wrapped in paper and tied with rubber bands across the desk to her, saying, "It's all there, two hundred thousand."

She picked up the package, peeling back the paper to peek at the money inside. "Wow!" she said, "I've never seen this much cash in my life."

"That is just the beginning," said Hector, "if you can get more of the product. Maybe someday I'll be working for you." he joked.

Lily laughed, and said, "I guess I'll let you get back to work."

"OK, Sally," said Hector, "I hope to see you soon."

"Until then..." said lily, rising to go with the package gripped firmly in her left hand. They shook hands and Lily practically ran out to the car.

Marsha backed out of the parking spot, started out onto the road, and asked, "How'd it go?"

"Awesome!" said Lily excitedly.

"That good, huh?" responded Marsha, "How much did you get?"

Lily looked over with a shit-eating grin. "two hundred thousand," she said, "with a promise of more when I make another trip."

Marsha turned to Lily with wide eyes, veering a little and breaking, provoking a blaring horn from the driver in the other lane. "Holy shit!" she said, "Those must be some antiques."

"Priceless, I think." said Lily. "The buyer was apparently very excited."

"I hope that's a good thing," said Marsha, "people are murdered and disappeared over that kind of money all the time. I can't tell you enough to be careful."

Lily could only say, "I know."

Flush with funds, Lily took Marsha out shopping, promising to buy her anything she wanted. Marsha gladly went along, but chose only a few modest articles of clothing and a fifty-two dollar bottle of her favorite perfume before declaring that Lily should save some money for a rainy day.

Lily also bought herself the latest I-phone, and pre-paid for a data and talk plan. The duo enjoyed lunch and a little wine at an upscale Italian restaurant. Then lily called up Amie, asking to take her shopping as repayment as well.

Marsha reluctantly dropped Lily off at Amie and Katie's, cautioning, "Don't let those two take advantage of you. They are not ones to exercise restraint, especially with someone else's money."

Lily assured her that she would be cautious, then knocked at the door to the apartment. Both Amie and Katie met her at the door, hugging her like a sister and inviting her in. They offered her a joint while she waited for them to finish getting ready, but she declined and drank some water.

The girls had a blast shopping, and Lily had never had as much fun in her life. By dinner, she had spent well over a thousand dollars for clothes, shoes, jewelry, the phone, food, and drink. After dinner, the girls dropped her back off at Marsha's, saying they had to get ready for the club.

Tired from the adventures of the past many days, Lily drank some herbal tea with Marsha, patted Bruno on the head, and went to bed. Marsha stayed up a little later, clicking on the TV to watch the ten-o-clock news. When the picture of Lily popped up on the screen behind the newscaster, Marsha did a double-take and leaned forward intently.

Then she went to her computer, searching out the story of the murders and the missing girl from Colorado. The headline read "Quadruple Homicide Rocks Rural Colorado Town". The article featured a video interview with San Miguel County Sherriff's Deputy James Sandborn at the top, with the original article and story updates below.

She clicked the start button on the video player, and a blonde female newscaster appeared in the window, saying, "...and breaking news out of Nucla Colorado. Authorities have begun a nationwide manhunt for seventeen-year old Lily DuCray, suspected in the murder of her step-father Jake Vigil and three other area men whose names are being withheld pending notification of relatives. Miss DuCray is believed to be armed and dangerous, and citizens are asked to avoid confrontation with her and instead call 911 if they have information about her whereabouts."

There, on the screen, was a clear shot of Lily, though she was younger and worse dressed. Marsha looked back toward the hallway and Lily's bedroom, but all was quiet.

"Shit!" she said, as the deputy came onto the screen, saying, "Miss DuCray is a troubled young woman whose mother had recently abandoned her, and she had recently been in trouble for bad behavior at school. It appears that her behavioral issues may have escalated to murder when her step-father attempted to discipline her. It is believed that she stole her step-father's gun, shooting the other men after being refused service at the local tavern."

The video ended, and she read through the rest of the article hastily:

Grand Junction, Colorado (KKCO, KKJC) Seventeen-year old Lily DuCray is being sought in connection with a quadruple homicide investigation in San Miguel County.

According to a press release from the San Miguel County Sherriff's office, Miss DuCray is suspected of shooting her step-father Jake Vigil seven times at point blank range with Mr. Vigil's own gun after being suspended from Nucla High School earlier that day.

Miss DuCray is then suspected of stealing a horse and travelling to nearby Naturita, where she was denied service at the local tavern. An altercation then occurred at the tavern, resulting in the shooting deaths of three additional men, whose names have not been released pending notification of relatives.

Miss DuCray is then alleged to have committed a carjacking,
which resulted in a fatal car crash which killed Montrose resident
Daniel Salvadore.

Lily DuCray's mother, 52 year old Sherry DuCray has since been
reported missing.

Anyone having information regarding this case or any other
serious crime is encouraged to call the San Miguel County Sherriff's
Department or Crime Stoppers.

Marsha sat back, a look of horror upon her face. Then she
ran outside and called 911 with Bruno bounding along behind
at her heels.

She did not read the two additional updates to the story.

Just as Lily lay down, her new phone rang. She sat up,
suddenly wakeful, and grabbed for it. It was an unknown
number, with no associated name, but her current registry of
phone numbers was very small, so she picked up.

"Hello?" she said apprehensively.

"Hey!" came the response from a vaguely familiar male
voice, "Uh, Sally?"

"Yeah," said Lily, "this is Sally."

"Yeah," came the voice, "Um, this is Leo."

"Hey Leo," said Lily, "what's up?"

"Yeah," said Leo, "Hey, we sure had a great time at that
party, huh?"

"Yeah, Leo," said Lily, "we sure did."

"Yeah!" returned Leo, "Hey, I was hopin' that maybe we
could get together again sometime, and party, or whatever."

"Yeah, Leo," said Lily unconvincingly, "sounds fun!"

"Yeah!" said Leo, "Hey, well maybe tonight? I could come
by and pick you up."

Lily sighed with her hand over the microphone, then said,
"OK Leo, see you in a few!" as cheerfully as she could. "How
did you get my number?" she asked, "I just got this phone
today."

"Yeah," said Leo, "Amie gave it to me."

"Cool," said Lily, "Bye!"

"Yeah!" said Leo, "Bye!"

Lily hung up and sat back on the bed for a minute, unsure whether she was scared or excited. She decided it was both and rose, heading back out to the kitchen. Marsha's laptop sat open on the counter, and a stupid commercial was on the TV, but Marsha was nowhere in sight.

She looked down the hall, but both the bathroom and Marsha's bedroom door were open, and unoccupied. She turned and saw the computer again, and her eyes widened.

"Oh, shit!" she cried, sitting down at the barstool long enough to confirm her fears.

Then she, too, ran out the door.

Leo pulled up in his Metallic blue BMW just as Lily saw an LAPD car pull around the corner into the apartment complex. She pulled on the door handle twice as he parked before he could un-lock the door, and she was in the car before he could even speak.

"Go, go, go, go!" she said with gritted teeth, and he complied, pulling back out to exit the lot.

"Yeah," said Leo as they passed the cop car and pulled onto the street, "Hey, what's up? Are you in trouble?"

"Yeah," Lily said, "I think so. I think the cops are after me."

Leo looked over at her, plainly checking her out. "Yeah," he said, "You don't got to worry about that. I'm gonna take you somewhere totally safe, and you don't gotta worry about it."

Lily's blood chilled. "What do you mean?" she asked.

"Hey," replied Leo a bit colder, "don't worry, you'll see."

Lily sat back ashen-faced and afraid.

"Hey," said Leo with a bit of false cheer, "I really like you. We ain't gonna hurt you."

"Then where are you taking me?" asked Lily as calmly as she could.

"Veracruz!" said Leo, "to see the El Toro."

"I don't understand," said Lily, "who is El Toro?"

"El Toro is the boss," said Leo, "I am taking you to him."

"Why?" asked Lily.

"I did not ask," said Leo, "but it is because of the gold you sold to Hector. El Toro says it is his heritage, and he wants all of it."

"I sold him all I had." said Lily.

"Yeah," said Leo, "but we know you can get more."

They drove straight to LAX, entering one of the many private terminals spread around the central hub and taxiways. Leo flashed a wave at the guard at the gate, and it rolled back to let them through, and they parked behind the second massive hanger.

"Hey," said Leo, "just stick with me, you'll be OK."

"OK, Leo," said Lily, "I'm counting on you."

They boarded the plane, a twin engine conventional Cessna, and taxied off to await their takeoff assignment. Lily looked around the cabin, and there was Hector and Martin, kicking back in comfortable-looking reclining seats.

"Hey, esses!" said Leo.

"What up, Leo?" asked Martin, "Hey Sally. Sit down, buckle up. Want anything to drink, smoke, coke?"

"No thanks, Martin." Lily replied, "Maybe a water."

"Suit yourself." Martin said, "Leo, get your girlfriend a water, huh?"

"OK, Martin." agreed Leo, and he turned to walk to the small pantry in the back of the plane.

Lily sat down in the seat next to Martin and looked over at him.

He settled comfortably in his seat and sipped some sort of amber cocktail, then said, "The easiest way this could go is you tell Leo and me where the rest of the treasure is stashed. Then me, and you, and Leo are all heroes when we fly in to Veracruz."

Lily stayed quiet, just watching Martin's face and hoping somehow that Leo would come through for her.

Martin glanced at Lily briefly, then continued, "Far more problematic is for us to just fly down there with nothing and try to negotiate."

"There is no treasure without me," said Lily, "and I think I might like Veracruz."

Martin shook his head, saying, "You are a brave girl, Lily."

Lily started at his use of her name, and she started to stammer a lame excuse, but he interrupted. "Do you think Hector just makes up IDs for everybody without first finding out who they really are? You are naïve, Lily DuCray. El Toro sells girls like you on the black market. Hell, Leo has had a couple dozen of them."

Martin looked up at Leo as he approached with a darkening expression, and continued, "Isn't that right, Leo?"

Leo glared at Martin, then handed a bottle of water to Lily. "Hey, here you go, Sally."

Lily looked up at Leo as he moved to take a seat across the narrow aisle.

"Hey," said Leo unconvincingly, "Martin's just fucking with you."

"Yeah," said Martin, "I was just fucking with you."

Lily shook her head and gritted her teeth and said, "Yeah, you are just fucking with me, huh?" The anger built in her and she stood, turning to face Martin and the others. "You fucking pieces of shit. You can just fucking take me to El fucking Toro. Nobody gets shit out of this without me!"

Leo rose and said, "Yeah, hey, nobody is trying to rip you off or hurt you. We're just supposed to take you to the boss. I'm sure you can work out some kind of deal. Just don't get greedy."

Lily glared at each of them in turn, and finally sat in the seat next to Leo. She looked over at him and said, "I guess I've always wanted to go to Mexico anyway. Are we going near the beach?"

"Yeah," said Leo, "It's pretty close to the beach. Be nice, and maybe we can go down there."

"Yeah, Leo," muttered Lily, "I'll be nice, while you fuck me and then fuck me over, just like my fucking step-brother wanted to do, and just like his fucking dad wanted to do. Are you gonna disappear me, like Martin says? Just like those other girls, huh, Leo? Just like fucking Jake did to my Mom!"

By then her voice had raised to a torn shriek, and the tears ran down her face. She looked at Leo again as he sat stoically trying to restrain his own anger.

"Shut the fuck up!" he said, and Lily could see that his eyes were watery with emotion, "I did what I had to do."

Lily looked back down, trying to quell the tears, and Hector spoke up, "Do you know who your girlfriend really is, Leo?"

Leo just looked across the aisle at Hector.

Hector continued, "Your little friend murdered her parents and three others in Colorado last week."

"Bullshit!" cried Lily, "That is total bullshit! My fucking step-father killed my Mom, and he would have killed me, too if I hadn't shot him first. My damn step-brother killed those other men for helping me."

From the intercom came a male voice, saying, "OK, everybody strap in, we are clear for takeoff." Then began the sudden acceleration and momentary vertigo as the plane took off. Hector pulled out his phone and sat back, reading something for a few minutes.

At length the pilot announced that they were free to move about the cabin. Leo's phone chirped a text notification, and he pulled it out and began to read as well.

Then Leo tapped Lily's arm, handing her his phone. "Hey," he said, "read this."

She took the phone and wiped her eyes with the back of her other hand. There on the screen was the same article she had seen on Marsha's computer. She sighed and lowered the phone, saying, "I saw, it says I'm a horrible serial killer loser."

Leo looked over at her and asked, "Did you read it?"

"I read enough." said Lily.

"Yeah, read it all," said Leo, "all the way to the bottom."

Lily scrolled down the page as she read the article she had earlier glimpsed. Below was another section heading reading:

Development:

Breaking news in the murders of Nucla and Naturita residents Jake Vigil, Peter Barnes, Daniel Weatherly, and Joseph Byne.

According to a Mesa County Sherriff's Department press brief, Sherriff's Department personnel recovered the handgun used in the slayings at the scene of a one-vehicle accident which killed Benjamin Vigil, the son of Jake Vigil, and critically injured Museum of the West Curator Miles Dunbury.

A body, believed to be that of Jake Vigil's common law wife, Sherry DuCray, was found at the bottom of a cliff in the Dolores River Canyon near Gateway, Colorado. The cause of death was not listed pending completion of an autopsy by the San Miguel County Coroner's office, but is considered suspicious by the San Miguel County Sherriff's Department.

Lily DuCray, Sherry DuCray's seventeen-year old daughter, who had been the prime suspect in the murders, is no longer considered a suspect, but is now considered a missing person. She may be attempting to travel to California via the I-70 corridor.

Benjamin Vigil, the deceased eighteen-year old football star at Nucla High School, is now suspected of the murder of his parents as well as Peter Barnes, Daniel Weatherly, and Joseph Byne.

Lily lowered the phone to her lap again, "Wow!" she said, "I find out I'm exonerated for murder from my Mexican Mafia kidnapper." She handed back the phone and added sincerely, "Thanks Leo."

Leo responded, "Yeah, no problem. Hey, I like you. I really hope everything works out OK."

"Me too," said Lily quietly.

They landed in Veracruz, and a limousine was waiting for them at the hanger. The driver said nothing as he opened the door for them and she got in, escorted by Leo and followed by Hector and Martin. She looked warily around at them before settling into the comfortable seat.

An uncomfortable silence reigned in the car as they left the airport and sped onto the highway, leaving the city behind. Gone was the arrogance and boisterousness the men had earlier displayed, and Lily saw that they were worried. She shook her head in resignation.

The ride lasted almost forty-five minutes, though it seemed to take much longer, and at last they pulled off the highway onto a rural road toward the sea. They stopped briefly at a gate, which opened at their approach, before pulling up into the circular driveway of a huge white and tan stucco mansion with red ceramic roof tiles.

The driver got out and opened the door for them again, and Martin was quick to exit, followed by Hector. Leo got out, offering a hand to Lily as she stepped out as well. Then the party turned and made their way to the big carved doors beneath the driveway awning.

Martin pushed a button beside the door, and it opened to a large foyer and huge tile-floor living room. Pre-Columbian art and relics were displayed prominently and tastefully throughout the room, though few matched the splendor of Lily's hoard.

A huge, thick-necked, burly man in a comfortable cotton guayabera shirt and tan trousers strode down the stairs as they entered, and the other men turned to him with obvious deference. "Hola, caballeros!" said El Toro. "Hector, Martin, Leo, me allegro de verte."

"Hola!" the men replied, "gracias, jefe."

Then Hector spoke as he stepped to the front and beckoned for Lily to come forward, "This is Miss Lily DuCray. Miss DuCray, meet El Toro."

Lily stepped forward tentatively, but El Toro strode to her confidently, taking her hand firmly in his massive hams and kissing it gently before saying, "Very pleased to meet you, Miss DuCray." He looked up at her over the back of her hand with bright, penetrating eyes and said, "I have heard a great deal about you, Miss DuCray."

Then he wrapped a massive arm around her shoulders and turned her toward the interior of the house, continuing, "First I hear that you are a hardened murderer of four or five strong men and your very own Mother, and that you have somehow acquired a small lot of very valuable relics of Azteca."

She looked up at him over her shoulder and his huge arm as she struggled to think of a response. "Then," he said, "I hear that you are just a naïve young girl who escaped her murderous step-brother and ran away to California, somehow acquiring a great quantity of very valuable relics of Azteca."

He looked down at her with a seemingly warm smile. "You are an enigma, Miss DuCray, full of secrets. Either way, I had to meet you for myself."

He led her into the living room, pausing in front of a wall display, where one of the famed Aztec solar disc calendars hung in a wooden frame. "The Aztec calendar," he said, "was a great feat of science to create." He looked at Lily's expression as he continued, "They could predict the dates of many astrological events far into their own future. They are said to have even predicted the coming of Cortez and the fall of their own civilization."

They strolled on, past a display of an ornate feathered costume of leather, fur and gold to a set of 16th century Spanish armor on a stand with a halberd in hand and a scabbarded sword on a belt. "All of this," he said, gesturing broadly at the many relics spread about the room, "tells a story. My story."

She looked back up at his face, and the smile had gone. Without looking back down to her, he said, "Now you will tell me of your story, so that I can see how you came to have such important artifacts of my story."

As she thought about what to say, he said, "Nos trae pulque, agua, y huachinango." and she noticed the white-clad raven-haired servant girl who had been lurking near the entry to the kitchen. Martin, Hector, and Leo were nowhere to be seen.

"Si, Senor Toro." said the girl as she scurried away.

He led Lily to the expensive cream-colored cotton couch, where he sat and beckoned for her to join him. "I want to hear all of your story, and you must leave nothing out."

She stared hard at him as he sat next to her, and she could see how he acquired his moniker, El Toro. Then she began to tell her story, trying hard to leave nothing out.

The servant girl reappeared shortly, bearing a big silver tray laden with two glasses of water, two glasses of an opaque light orange colored drink with a white frothy head, and two plates with a paprika fish filet garnished with colorful mango, parsley, olives, and capers, served with small potatoes, and rice.

The scent of garlic in olive oil wafted in with the sweet odor of the mango as the girl placed the tray on the coffee table in front of them. Lily saw the look of familiar terror in the girl's eyes as they briefly crossed gazes, and she shuddered as the girl cowed before them before fled back toward the kitchen.

She did not yet know that his full nickname, which was never used in his presence, was El Toro Loco Diablo. It was some time before she would learn why.

Chapter 23: Showdown

They talked late into the night, and El Toro listened intently to her story, asking poignant questions when a detail caught his attention. He did not question her dream about Enrico's adventures, seeming to consider the vision as historic truth.

At the end of her story, in the wee hours of the morning, El Toro said, "We will fly to Grand Junction soon, and you will take me to the museum, to confirm what you have told me. Then we will go to the Grand Mesa and recover the rest of what Fray De La Cruz stole from my people."

Lily looked at his hard features for a moment before saying, "I am still wanted by the authorities in Colorado, and the people at the museum know me."

"My people will disguise you," replied El Toro with certitude, "and they will never know you are there. You will remain silent while we are there, so that your friends there will be safe."

Lily looked at his set jaw, and nodded cooperatively, saying, "Of course."

"Buenos noches, Lily DuCray." he said, "I will see you in the morning."

At that, he rose and walked to the stairs without a backward glance, climbing them easily despite his great bulk. When he had gone, the servant girl came in and beckoned Lily to follow.

The girl led Lily up the stairs to another hall and a very well-appointed room decorated in tasteful tan and white Mexican style. "I'm Lily," said Lily as she followed, "what is your name?"

The girl half-turned and shook her head, then turned to leave. Lily tried again, "Me nombre es Lily. ¿Que es su nombre?"

Again, the girl half-turned, and Lily saw raw fear in her eyes as she shook her head again and held a finger up to her lips.

Lily shut up and watched as she left and shut the door behind her. Just to check, she tried turning the doorknob, but she was locked in. Exhausted, she stripped to her underwear and crawled into the comfortable big bed.

The next morning, she awoke as the servant girl opened her door and came in, saying, "Buenos dias, Senora Lily."

Lily sat up in the bed, saying, "Buenos dias, senorita." The girl laid a bundle of clothes on the dresser, and Lily said, "Gracias! Su tenga me nombre, que es su nombre?"

"Rosaria, senora." the servant girl said quietly. "Usted puede tomar una ducha en el baño en el pasillo. Luego se unirá a El Toro para desayunar en la veranda."

After High School Spanish and her long dream of Enrico, Lily understood most of what Rosaria said, so she nodded, "Si, Gracias Rosaria."

Rosaria responded, "De nada." closed the door and scurried off, leaving Lily to look through the clothes she had been brought. First, she picked up a lovely traditional Mexican dress of white cotton, with colorful embroidered flowers and stylized animals. There also was a soft white robe, a lime-green bikini, and huarache sandals.

She put on the robe and bundled the rest beneath her arm, making her way to the hall bathroom, which was tiled in salmon and gray, with and oversized shower and spa tub. Thick, soft rugs covered the floor in front of the tub, toilet, shower, and bath, and she relished the feel of the rugs on her feet.

She took care of her morning purge, and had a long, thorough shower where she shaved her legs and trimmed her pubic hair. Then she donned the bikini, dress, and huaraches, and proceeded down to the dining room, where Leo, Hector, Martin, and El Toro sat.

The table was heaped with a pot of fresh chicory coffee, a plate of enpanadas, eggs, and fried potatoes, and an assortment of local fruit including mango, banana, and strawberry.

"Buenos dias, Lily!" said El Toro with a broad smile. "Come and Join us for breakfast."

"Gracias, Senor!" said Lily with as much enthusiasm as she could fake. "It smells wonderful!" she added honestly."

"It is delicious!" said El Toro as he patted the empty seat next to him, "Come, sit."

Lily obeyed, hungrily eyeing the heaps of food. Rosaria appeared as if from nowhere, a pitcher in her hand. "¿Popo, Senora?" she asked.

Lily wasn't sure what popo was, but she nodded and answered, "Si, gracias."

Rosaria filled a small round wooden cup with a somewhat viscous frothy brown liquid, handing it to Lily. Lily took the cup carefully to avoid spilling, saying, "Gracias, Rosaria.", before taking a sip. The drink was a delicious lightly sweetened chocolate flavor with un undertone of rice, cinnamon, and anise. "Mmm," she said, "I've never tried popo before."

"It is a treat, a specialty of Veracruz." said El Toro, "I am glad you enjoy it."

The group dined in silence for a few moments, with small talk primarily about the delicious regional foods. Then El Toro spoke up, "There are a great many wonderful things to do and see here in Veracruz."

He took a bite of his empanada, chewed, and swallowed before continuing, "Leo would like to take you out to see the sights today if you are interested."

Lily sipped her coffee and looked at Leo, who was trying to smile reassuringly. "That sounds wonderful," she said, "thank you, Leo."

"Yeah!" said Leo, "you're welcome. We could go to the beach, or shopping, or whatever."

"Yeah," said Lily, "whatever sounds great." She looked back to El Toro briefly, adding, "Aren't there some interesting historical and archaeological sites near here as well?"

"Yeah!" said Leo, "uh..."

"There are indeed a great many interesting historic archaeological sites near here." said El Toro, "I believe your Enrico traveled through here on his way north." He took a sip of popo, and added, "I am gratified at your interest in my history, Lily."

Lily chewed thoughtfully for a moment, saying, "Thank you. I've always found the subject fascinating, especially in light of my dream."

Lily opted to visit the beach first, which was an easy kilometer walk from the mansion. Lily was not surprised to see guards with assault rifles at key points patrolling the grounds. Leo said little, strolling along beside Lily while plainly trying to maintain his poker face.

"Thanks for taking me out and about today, Leo." said Lily.

"Yeah," said Leo, "No problem."

Lily walked for a few minutes in silence, enjoying the stroll along the lawn on the terrace above the sea, with the jungle not far to each side. "How many other girls have you fucked and taken out on a last outing, Leo?"

Leo swallowed hard, flashing a hard glance her way and setting his jaw. "Hey," he said defensively, "Come on, I didn't know anything about you when we got together. How should I know you were a virgin with millions of dollars' worth of black market shit the boss wants? You gonna take my gun and shoot me, too?"

"I don't want to shoot you, Leo." said Lily. "When I met you at the party, I didn't know what I wanted... but I know I didn't want to be killed or abducted, and I didn't want to be a disposable sex toy for a bunch of gangsters."

They had reached the top of the bluff overlooking the beach, and a steep trail led down to the strand. Lily trotted down the trail in silence, with Leo hurrying along behind. For a moment she just stood and stared at the scene with a strange sense of deja-vu. Then she took off her huaraches and dress at the base of the sea cliffs, setting them on a rock before running into the low surf.

She splashed and played in the waves for a few minutes somewhat joylessly as Leo followed her back and forth from the dry sand farther up the beach. Finally, Leo stripped off his shirt, shoes, and trousers, leaving them on the rocks near Lily's clothes. Then he ran into the surf to join her, taking her in his arms as he caught her.

She thrilled at his touch, and returned the embrace, reveling in the feel of his muscular young body pressed up against her mostly naked self. She trembled despite the warm sun and water, pulling back to touch his chest and strong shoulders.

Then he kissed her again, only her second real kiss, and she felt her anger melting away into something else. Her eyes were wet when she looked back up into his soft brown eyes.

"I have never felt this way about anyone before," said Leo, "and I have never been with a virgin before, either. I don't know what will happen once El Toro gets what he wants, but I won't let anyone hurt you, OK?"

"OK, Leo," said Lily. "I've never felt this way about anyone before either, but there's a whole lot of things I've done and felt lately that I never felt before." Her pussy tingled, as if in agreement, and she pressed herself to him tightly.

"Is there someplace private we can go?" she asked as they waded back out of the water.

Leo looked around at the empty beach and said, "This is El Toro's private beach. No-one will disturb us."

Lily glanced around briefly to confirm his statement, enjoying the view with less of the cloud of uncertainty and fear with which she had originally seen it. Then she smiled a genuine Lily DuCray smile at him, and his hard heart melted even more.

For a moment the whole scene seemed surreal, and she remembered Rico and Nahana embracing in the surf after their wedding. It was the very same beach, she was sure of it. She trembled and hoped she and Leo would fare better than Rico and Nahana had.

This time they made love deliberately, without any of the false desperation of the cocaine. They took their time, fully exploring each other there on the wide, thick, cotton towel in the warm Caribbean sun. When they were sated they napped for a while listening to the surf and gulls.

They fetched masks, fins, and snorkels from the mansion and returned to the beach, where they spent the rest of the morning swimming along the reef. The time seemed to race by as they watched the colorful fish dart among the brightly colored variegated corals.

Too soon, they had to be on their way if they were to make it to Veracruz Plaza's markets and museum, so they plodded back to the mansion and drove to Veracruz in one of El Toro's open-top jeeps. They ate a light, tasty meal at a little shop on the plaza, and then toured the museum.

The many Spanish and Pre-Columbian relics made the nape of her neck crawl, and the whole experience took on the quality of a dream. She imagined the endless grim parade of dead since the first incursions by Europeans into the New World. As she read the accounts of the Conquest, she began to feel uneasy, and asked Leo if he would take her back to the estate.

As they drove, Lily turned to Leo and said, "I could just let him have all of it, if he just lets us go free. I just need enough money to get by."

Leo glanced over at her and drove on in silence for a moment before saying, "He would probably agree, and we would go off smiling… but then he would have us killed."

"Why?" Lily asked, "We are no threat to him."

"He sees everyone as a threat to him." said Leo. "The only people who meet him and live are those who work for him."

"I guess we either work for him or kill him, then." Lily said flatly. "I'm already a murderer, so..."

"When the time comes," Leo interrupted, "I will kill him."

Lily looked over at him, plainly gauging his honesty. "We will kill him," she said at last, "if we must.".

They finished the drive in relative silence, and were ushered to the big dining room table by Rosaria as soon as they arrived. They joined El Toro, Hector, and Martin amid dinner.

"There they are!" said El Toro, "just like two lovebirds returning to the nest." He gestured to the two open seats next to him, saying, "Sit down, have a margarita or some popo. Tonight, we are having Steak Veracruz. It is very delicious."

When they had sat down, Rosaria served them each a thin steak covered in a tomato olive habanero sauce with onions and green peppers, rice, and beans, and poured them each a margarita from a pitcher on the table.

"What did you find in your adventures today, Leo?" asked El Toro. "Did you show our young Lily the museum and plaza?"

Leo swallowed a sip of his margarita before beginning to answer, "Yeah, um…"

"Veracruz is amazing!" interrupted Lily, "Especially the museum and the plaza. This place is thick with history." She smiled as sweetly as she could manage and cut a bite from her steak, chewing it with apparent relish.

El Toro looked from Leo to Lily and back again. "Yes!" he said, "I am gratified to see that you have reconciled. Leonardo is a good kid, for a Chichimec."

Lily glanced sidelong at Leo, smiled at El Toro again, and said, "Leo and I are getting along great together, and I'm really very fond of him. He is my first real boyfriend."

"Ah," exclaimed El Toro expansively, "What a joy it is to be young and in love." He deliberately ate another bite of his meal and added, "I know you had not planned on this trip to Veracruz, but we will take care of our business very soon, and you will be free to do as you please."

Lily tried to make her fake smile appear as real as she could as she said, "That is good, I'm sure my roommate is worried about me."

El Toro turned to face her directly, saying, "Marsha is very worried about you." Her face fell despite her efforts at El Toro's mention of Marsha's name, and he continued, "She will be fine, I'm sure." He sipped some popo from his cup, wiped the froth from his lip, and added, "All we have to do before you can get back to her is finish our business here and in Colorado."

Lily took a swig of her margarita, smiled again, and said, "Sounds great! It really is very nice here, and it shouldn't take too terribly long to do what we need to do in Colorado."

"It is time we come to terms, then." said El Toro as he waved a huge hand to dismiss the others. "Give us some privacy, gentlemen."

The others rose quickly and left the table without a word, heading back outside into the humid, warm air as Lily and El Toro stood and watched. Then El Toro beckoned, saying, "Come, let us sit." He led her upstairs and down the hall to a balcony overlooking the path to the sea.

They sat on white wicker chairs in the pale light of a gibbous moon as the last light of sunset faded away. "I will give you one million dollars for the rest of the treasure," said El Toro, "and you will never speak of it to another person, upon pain of death."

Lily nodded slowly and said, "I know that the treasure is worth many, many times that amount of money." El Toro's eyes narrowed just a bit, and she added, "I will accept three million, with proof that Marsha is OK and assurances that you won't just have me killed and take back the money."

"I was told that you were naïve, Lily DuCray." said El Toro. "Murder and life on the run have a way of ripping away such naivete." He paused for dramatic effect and added, "Two million dollars."

Lily shook her head. "Three million," she said, "and proof that Marsha is OK and not in a position to be held hostage. One million now, in an account only I can access. The other two million in cash before we leave for Colorado."

El Toro stared hard at her for a few moments and said, "We have a deal."

They drove to the airport early the next morning in the limo. El Toro was uncharacteristically jovial, and the mood proved contagious. The whole party smiled and joked and laughed throughout the ride and boarding, only quieting as the plane raced to take off.

The plane soared to altitude and leveled off, but the captain piped through the speakers, "I recommend that everyone remain in their seats throughout this flight, as we are likely to experience some turbulence."

The trip took only two and a half hours, and soon enough they were descending through thick clouds with many bumps and jolts as the plane fought the storm. They could barely see the runway before the landing gear chirped and bumped upon the asphalt.

The plane taxied past the main terminal to the area where the private planes were tied or hangered, finally stopping near one of the larger hangers. When the co-pilot opened the cabin door, the wind slammed the door against the side of the plane with a loud bang, and a light, cold mist blew through the cabin.

Soon enough, the crew had the stairs in place, and they descended through a driving rain to the tarmac. They all hurried to the hanger, entering through a side door and travelling down a hall to another exit on the other side of the building, where two rental Escalades awaited.

"Leo," said El Toro, tossing him the key fob, "you drive, Lily and I will ride with you."

Leo clicked open the doors with a double chirp from the vehicle, and El Toro climbed into the big back seat, telling Lily, "You get the Navigator's seat." When she got in he said, "Let us go to the museum, then we should stop somewhere for food and whatever tools we may need. Tell Leo where to go."

Lily directed them to the museum, while she donned a black, curly wig and some makeup provided by Hector. Then El Toro led them in and paid Molly the receptionist, also buying a topographic map of the Grand Mesa National Forest. Lily was careful to keep her face out of sight of the volunteer despite the disguise.

When El Toro was done in the gift shop, Lily led them on a tour of the museum, making special note of the discoveries along Kannah Creek and the other Spanish Conquest related displays. She also pointed out the likely route of the Aztec migration south and the route Rico's party took north.

During her explanations, she got a bit overexcited, and Leo put a hand on her shoulder as he noticed the receptionist look over curiously.

"We should go now." said Leo, "The receptionist was looking at you funny."

Lily glanced over at Molly and agreed, and they all made their way out, the men taking care to block the receptionist's view. They piled back into the vehicles and hurried away.

Lily took them to Murdoch's, where they purchased rain gear, two shovels, a pick, and a pry-bar, as well as several heavy-duty PVC utility boxes, straps, and padlocks.

"There is no way we can carry all this out in one trip." Lily said as she helped load the equipment into the hatchback of the SUV. "We will have to make several trips or rent pack horses."

"Do you know where we can rent horses?" asked El Toro.

"I think so," replied Lily, "but I need to call and make sure."

She searched on-line on her phone for a few minutes and found the Fischer's phone number, which she dialed with the press of the green phone icon.

Mrs. Fischer answered, "Hello, this is the Fischer's."

"Hi Mrs. Fischer," said Lily, "is Bob around?"

"He's in the other room," said Mrs. Fischer, "Just a moment. "Bob!" she called away from the phone, "Phone call."

Bob picked up a few moments later, saying, "Bob Fischer. What can I do for you?"

"Hi Bob!" said Lily, "I was wondering if you could rent me three pack horses."

"Lily," said Bob with obvious concern, "is that you?"

"Yeah!" said Lily, "Hi Bob! Some friends and I were just gonna go up to the mountain for a couple days and we were hoping we could rent some horses."

"You sure picked some lousy camping weather!" said Bob, "It's supposed to rain cats and dogs for the next couple of days." He beckoned to his wife to come closer, mouthing, "Lily DuCray! Use your cell and call the Sherriff."

"Oh yeah?" said Lily, "That's too bad. My friends are only in town for a few days and they really have their hearts set on the mountain, so…"

The pause grew uncomfortable but finally Bob said, "Well I'm sure I can get some horses ready for you. When do you want to head out?"

"Thank you so much!" said Lily, "We'd like to get going as soon as possible. Today if we can."

Another long pause preceded, "Better give me at least an hour. You need a trailer?"

"If it's not too inconvenient," said Lily, "Could you meet us at Kannah Creek Trailhead?"

"Sure." said Bob, "Not a problem. See you at about eleven am."

"Thanks!" said Lily, "Sounds great!"

They stopped at the Denny's near Murdoch's and ate brunch while watching the rain pour down. The gutters ran with brown turbid water as the storm drains struggled to accommodate the rare heavy rain. The exuberance they had shared earlier faded to a vague trepidation and they said little as they ate and sipped coffee.

The drive to the trailhead took about forty minutes with the windshield wipers flailing against the storm. The gravel parking lot was sodden and the three horses stood with their backs to the wind where they were tied in the lee of the Fischer's four-horse fifth-wheel trailer and white Dodge dually.

Bob got out of the cab at their approach, and Lily got out as soon as they stopped. With a nod, El Toro told Leo to stay with her.

"Hi Bob!" said Lily as cheerfully as she could from beneath the hood of her raincoat, "Wet enough for ya?"

"You are out of your mind to go camping on a day like this." said Bob as Leo walked around the Escalade to join them. "Take it easy on the horses. That trail can be slippery as hell in places when it gets this wet."

"We'll be extra careful." Said Lily. "We should be back by tomorrow evening. I've got cash on me now if you'd like."

"Nah," replied Bob, "no hurry. I'll just get it from you when you get back tomorrow. Eighty bucks per horse per day, plus any damages."

"No problem, Bob." Lily said. "I guess we'll see you then."

"OK," he said, "Be careful out there."

He walked back to his truck and got back in as Lily checked out the horses and tack. Leo stood behind her looking somewhat miserable beneath his rain hood.

When the dodge pulled the trailer out of the lot and headed back down the road, El Toro, Martin and Hector got out of the vehicles and joined them at the horses. None of them had ever horse-packed before, and though Lily was quite experienced with horses, it still took considerable trial and error to stow the equipment and containers on the pack horses.

At last they set out plodding through the mud up the slippery trail, with Lily, Leo, and Martin each leading a horse. El Toro stayed close to Lily at the front of the column, and Hector followed along behind. All was quiet save for the patter of the rain on the leaves and ground.

The creeks which had been but little trickles and streams were now rushing torrents as they bounded down the mountain over boulders and logs. Where before she had easily leapt across or stepped across on rocks, now they were forced to wade.

El Toro plowed through the rushing stream with relative ease, but behind him, little Lily's feet were swept out from under her and she plunged into the cold water. The strong current bashed her legs against several rocks as it dragged her along its course, but she kept her grip on the lead rope and the horse kept her from being dragged away.

El Toro plunged back into the stream, grabbing her by the arm and dragging her to the bank, where she regained her footing. "Wow!" she said between splutters, "Thanks!"

El Toro responded, "You are very welcome, my Dear."

The others crossed the creek even more carefully, and in a few hours, they left the trail, fighting through the wet brush up the slope to the cave. At the mouth, Lily unpacked the horses while the others explored. When Lily took up a shovel and began to dig, El Toro nodded to the other men, and they took over.

Lily stepped back with El Toro to watch as she shivered in her soaked clothes. "There is a mark on the top of the shelf there that matches a mark on the map I found in Dry Creek."

"Where is this map?" asked El Toro. "I would like to see it."

"All I have is a copy." said Lily, "The original, the letters, and the scroll-case are at the museum." She dug into her wet pocket below the raincoat and extracted the worn, sodden, folded copies of the map and letters. "I hadn't meant for these to be the only copies I had, but..."

She handed the wet paper to El Toro just as Leo's shovel clunked against the buried flagstones. Leo extracted the flagstones and brushed away some loose dirt.

"There it is!" she said with more trepidation than excitement. Leo and Martin cleared away the dirt more carefully, and extracted the chest Lily had earlier opened.

El Toro's huge hands trembled with excitement mirrored in the expressions of the other men as he stepped over, knelt, and opened the chest. He lifted a few of the precious items in his huge hands and replaced them with reverence, closing the chest as he rose. "Is there more?" asked El Toro as he turned and nodded to Hector.

"Yes," replied Lily, "but I didn't get a chance to check it out."

Hector and El Toro hefted the heavy chest, carefully settling it into the PVC box on one of the horses as Leo and Martin kept digging.

When they dragged out the rotten oilcloth and began to investigate the bundle, El Toro said, "Leave the bundle intact. We will look at it later." He and Hector hefted the bundle and began to secure it to the horse while Leo and Martin dug out another smaller chest. This, too was placed within the other PVC box on the third horse.

"I think that is all of it." said Lily, shivering. "We should go."

Martin turned to her and said, "We should keep digging, there might be even more!"

El Toro looked at Lily, then turned to Martin, saying "No, this is all of it. Let's go."

They walked and slid with the overloaded horses down the steep, slippery grass, mud, and brush covered slope. Hector cursed as his feet slid out from under him and he landed in the mud, sliding fifteen or twenty feet downhill and crashing into the oak brush. Martin, Leo, and El Toro laughed as he scrambled to his feet and wiped his muddy hands on his raincoat.

"Can't keep your hands clean this time, huh Hector?" asked Martin.

"Fuck you, Martin." spluttered Hector.

"Some other time," laughed Martin, "you're a mess."

Even Lily snickered despite her shivering. Soon they reached the little torrent they had waded earlier, and it had grown even more perilous.

El Toro beckoned to Lily, saying, "Give me your hand. I'll take the reins and help you across."

"OK," said Lily, putting her little hand in his.

They waded out into the powerful current, and El Toro's strong grip hurt Lily's wrist and hand. Still she had to struggle to retain her footing amid the slippery cobbles. Then El Toro said, "Adios, Lily DuCray." and shoved her by the arm into the worst of the torrent, where she was swept quickly away.

With a loud "Bang!" Leo shot El Toro in the back. El Toro staggered forward, turning and trying to stand in the wild stream, and the horse bolted back toward the trailhead. Martin and Hector reached into their raincoats for their pistols, but the other two horses jostled them as they raced after the first, also spoiling Leo's second shot.

Leo leapt from the path and bounded as fast as he could downslope alongside the tumbling brook. He looked for Lily as he went, tearing his raincoat on a branch in the thick brush. Then he saw just a splash of her red rain jacket far below in the midst of a brush-covered snag blocking the stream like a great sieve.

He ran the rest of the way down and fought through the thick foliage to the brush dam. He could see part of the jacket below a fallen tree and pile of brush. As he clambered dangerously into the brush pile, the little glimpse of the red jacket disappeared below the waves.

When he reached the water, he plunged his arm in and probed around, but there was nothing but brush and twigs. He crept more carefully back out of the torrent and stared blankly downstream. Nothing could live through that, he thought. He shook his head miserably and struggled not to cry.

Unsure of the topography, Leo stealthily crept back up the slope some distance back from the stream. He waited and watched for a moment when he regained sight of the trail and stream crossing, but nobody was in sight.

Then Leo followed the others back toward the trailhead as stealthily as he could, and he kept his pistol at the ready.

Lily reeled back at El Toro's shove and was instantly swept away. She slammed into the rocks, and the brush and limbs tore at her clothes and hair. She heard a distant "Bang!" amid the roar of the rushing water over stones.

She was battered and tossed about with little possibility of escape for what seemed to her a long time, then she crashed into a pile of brush in the stream. In a second, the water pressure shoved her through the brush, stripping off her torn jacket and ejecting her back into the stream below.

She kept her feet downstream as best she could, and caught her breath at every safe opportunity. Soon the little torrent poured into a bigger one, and she was swept along with it. At long last she was able to catch hold of the bank in the lee of a large boulder, and she crawled out of the stream.

She lay shivering for some time, too weary and cold to continue. Then she rose and began making her way upslope where she knew she would eventually find the trail again. Then she heard the unmistakable sound of horse's hooves trotting, so she whistled and hurried faster toward the sound.

Not far ahead stood all three horses on the trail looking toward her with lead ropes trailing and loads somewhat askew. She nickered at them and they ambled over to her. She quickly straightened out the loads and secured the horses in a tether line, finishing just as Martin came into view behind them.

She ducked to the front of the horses hoping he had not seen her, snatched up the lead rope again and began to run as fast as she could with her bruised and battered body on the muddy, uneven trail. She heard the bang of Martin's pistol behind her and had to duck to the side as the horses began to run again.

As the last horse passed, she swung up on his back somewhat clumsily and he staggered and slipped a bit with the sudden uneven weight. Then she pulled herself up onto his back and they trotted away from Martin through the trees.

At the trail junction leading to the little roadside park, she tried to stop the horses with a "Whoa! Whoa, boys." but the horses kept on trotting.

Then she caught the first glimpse of the parking lot and her cold body chilled even further. The lot was filled with Sherriff's Department and other law enforcement vehicles with horse trailers and horses. She froze for a second, then detached the cinch on the load, carefully balancing to avoid tipping it.

As soon as she could, she slid off the horse downslope and pulled off the PVC container behind her. She was unable to compensate for the speed and uneven, plunging slope, and she tumbled down it below the trail. The heavy PVC box tumbled after her, furrowing the ground and dumping out the smaller chest to roll farther down the hill.

She lay dazed for some time, and heard the sounds of voices.

Martin said, "They have mounted cops getting ready to come up here. We could try to cut through the brush and walk out, but it is a very long walk back to town. Maybe we can steal a truck, or something."

Hector replied, "We could just ditch the guns and claim we are just undocumented visitors who got lost in the woods and were shot by a crazy person."

El Toro said, "Yes, Bob Fischer has turned on his friend Lily. We will just load our camping gear into the cars and then answer a few questions. Lily just shot me when she saw the cops. No-one will ever know."

"What about Leo?" said Hector, "He will rat us out for what happened to his girlfriend."

"We kill him." said El Toro simply. "Set up an ambush. If the mounties get to us before Leo, we ditch the guns and get out."

Lily crept back up the slope and peeked up the trail, watching as the men set up to ambush Leo. Soaking wet, chilled to the bone, battered, bruised, and unarmed, she could not fight three strong men. She turned and ran all the way back to the parking lot.

Lily ran around a bend near the parking lot, slipped, and fell just as she came into view of the first of the three mounted Sherriff's Deputies.

"Whoa!" yelled the Deputy, "Hold it right there, Miss DuCray!"

Lily froze, sitting in the mud. "You've got to help me!" she cried. "Those men tried to kill me, and they are going to kill my friend! You've got to hurry."

The Deputies rode over to her, as the second one spoke into his lapel radio microphone, "This is Deputy Crenshaw. We have Miss DuCray here. It looks like we need medical assistance."

The first Deputy dismounted and helped Lily to her feet. "You don't have any weapons or drugs on you, do you?"

"No, Sir." said Lily, "Please, you've got to help my friend. They are going to murder him."

"Who are these men?" asked the Deputy as he frisked her cursorily.

"Some Mexican Mafia guys named El Toro, Martin, and Hector. They tried to kill me and they're trying to kill my boyfriend Leo."

The second Deputy spoke into his lapel mic again, saying, "Requesting backup, Miss DuCray reports three armed suspects are planning to ambush another individual."

The voice came back on the radio, "Hold your position and wait for backup. Do not approach the suspects."

"Ten four." replied the Deputy.

Lily tried to break away from the Deputy, but he gripped her wrist and put his hand on his gun and tazer. "Don't make me taze you, Miss DuCray."

She stopped struggling and put her head down. "So, you can't help him." she said softly.

"We'll see what we can do." replied the Deputy.

The second Deputy spoke into his mic again, "Miss DuCray claims the three suspects present an immediate threat to another individual. We request permission to proceed."

After a moment of silence, the radio returned, "Understood, proceed with extreme caution."

"Ten four," replied the Deputy.

"The medical team will be right here, Miss DuCray." said the first Deputy.

"It is an ambush," said Lily, "let me go with you at least until we're close so I can show you where they hid."

The Deputies looked at one another, and the leader said, "OK, Miss DuCray. I am Deputy Martinez, this is Deputy Warren, and this is Deputy Crenshaw. Where are these men planning the ambush?"

"They're probably about half a mile to a mile farther in." said Lily. "I can let you know when we get close."

"Make sure to stop us before we get in sight or hearing of the suspects." said Deputy Martinez.

Martinez remounted his horse and helped Lily climb up behind him. Then the group moved on up the trail until Lily thought they were getting close to the ambush site.

"Stop here." she said quietly, "They are just around the next bend. There are two guys uphill to the right, and another below the trail to the left."

"Wait here," said Martinez as he dismounted, "the medical team should be right behind us."

The other Deputies dismounted as well, and Crenshaw pulled a rifle from its holster alongside the saddle, saying, "I'll find a good spot and check in when I'm in place."

"OK," said Martinez, "I'll get eyes on him and wait for your signal."

Crenshaw headed upslope through the trees and Martinez advanced along the trail carefully, stopping behind some oak brush at the point of the bend in the trail and looking around with binoculars. Deputy Warren followed along at a distance, staying in sight of both Lily and Martinez as he passed out of Lily's view.

All was quiet except for the near constant drizzle of rain upon the leaves. Then she heard distant voices, though she could not catch the words. A gunshot rang out, then another, and two more in quick succession.

"Officer down!" shouted Deputy Warren into his mic as he ran toward Martinez around the bend.

Lily bolted up the trail as fast as she could run, rounding the corner and slipping in the mud. The slip saved her, though, as she heard another gunshot and the bark of the tree behind her erupted from the impact.

Ahead lay Deputy Warren, groaning as he crawled into the cover at the trailside. Beyond lay Deputy Martinez sprawled in the trail. El Toro lay just beyond him, and she saw Martin running down the slope diagonally toward her with his pistol in hand.

Lily ran forward, diving toward Martinez as he lay sprawled. His gun lay near his hand, and she snatched it up, rolling to face Martin and firing. Martin faltered, clutching at his chest, then fell face first to slide and roll into the ditch beside the trail.

Deputy Warren sat up where he had crawled beside the trail, aiming his pistol at something behind Lily below the trail. She turned and saw Hector, empty hands raised in surrender, walking slowly up to the trail. "Don't shoot!" he said, "I give up!"

Lily aimed Martinez's pistol at Hector, saying, "Where is Leo?"

Hector shook his head and said, "I don't know. After he shot El Toro and ran off, we didn't see him again."

Deputy Warren kept his gun trained on Hector, but said, "Put down the gun, Miss DuCray. We've got this under control."

Lily shook her head, and Hector said, "I never wanted to hurt you, Lily. You know that. I always tried to help you."

"Yeah," said Lily icily, "You helped feed me to the wolves."

"I did what I had to." said Hector. "I am very sorry."

The sound of more horses came to them from the direction of the trailhead, and another six riders came into view. They dismounted near Lily and Warren, and some hustled over to Martinez, Martin, and El Toro while another Deputy handcuffed Hector and read him his rights.

Lily looked around at the fallen men, sat back in the mud, and cried. She barely listened as the paramedics came and crouched down beside her, examining her many wounds and loading her onto a stretcher.

She fell asleep as they carried her out bundled under dry blankets on the litter.

Chapter 25: A Place in the Sun

She awoke the next day in the hospital, and was shocked to see all the many arrangements of flowers with cards displayed around her room. There at her bedside sat Mrs. Chisholm, and she smiled at Lily when Lily opened her eyes.

"I'm glad to see you awake." said Mrs. Chisholm. "You've had a rough time of it, but you're safe now. The authorities know all about Ben and Jake now, and the kidnappers are dead or in jail. You just rest now. When they let you out of the hospital, you can come live with us while we sort out the situation if you like.'

Tears came to Lily's eyes afresh, and she smiled at Mrs. Chisholm. "Thank you!" she croaked through her dry throat.

"I'm sorry to hear what happened to Redwing." said Mrs. Chisholm, "and your poor Mother. She deserved better. You deserve better."

Lily nodded, but could not bring herself to answer. Finally, she asked, "What about my friend Leo?"

Mrs. Chisholm shook her head, saying, "I don't know anything about anyone named Leo. Maybe you can ask Deputy Warren. He says you saved him from one of the gangsters and has been asking to see you. Two of the gangsters are dead, and the other one is in custody."

Lily nodded and reached for the prettiest flower arrangement, a bundle of multicolored flowers with a card in an envelope clipped onto a spike.

Mrs. Chisholm picked up the arrangement and handed it to Lily, saying, "It really is lovely that so many people have heard about your story and sent flowers and cards. You went from villain to celebrity since we last met."

Lily took the flowers, turning the arrangement to look at all sides and sniffing at the blooms with half-closed eyes.

"The artifacts you recovered made world news," said Mrs. Chisholm, "the biggest find of Aztec treasure outside Mexico. Mrs. Dunham says her husband can hardly stand being cooped up in here when he could be examining all the new relics."

Lily opened the envelope and pulled out the card, trembling as she saw the image. "Viva Veracruz!" read the flowy text above a lovely picture of the Plaza and museum. She burst into tears of joy when she read the message:

To my sweet Lily DuCray,

Hola from Mexico! The trip back to Veracruz was quick and a bit too exciting. The package you left along the trail is here for you whenever you need it.

Please accept this invitation to our new estate in Veracruz. We have a wedding to plan, if you are willing.

With Love and best wishes for a quick recovery,

Leo.

The wind tussled Leo's short, black curls into his face as he watched Lily approach down the red carpet rolled out along the beach. She wore a beautifully embroidered but simple white cotton dress with a lily in her hair as Sam Chisholm led her slowly toward him where he waited with the priest. Behind Lily, dressed in slightly less intricate embroidered colorful cotton dresses came Sarah Dunbury, Marsha, and Amie.

At Leo's side beneath the white, lily strewn gazebo stood Miles Dunbury, dressed similarly to Leo in a white, embroidered guayabera, black pants, and boots. In the small audience was Mrs. Chisholm, most of Leo's staff, and volunteers and employees of the Museum of Western Colorado and the Museo de Cera de Veracruz.

Lily and Leo had brokered an exhibit sharing between the two museums, and the discussions had been exciting to the scientists and historical hobbyists from both institutions at the rehearsal dinner the night before. Leo had donated the smaller chest to the Museo at Lily's request, but Lily still had the three million she had gotten from El Toro.

Also at Lily's request, Leo had divested all of the nefarious industries El Toro had been involved in for just enough to afford the estate and a modest lifestyle. He still kept armed guards, but was no longer the target he would otherwise have been.

At last, Lily stepped up on the low platform with him and they turned to face one another and join hands. He barely heard the words of the priest as he recited them, but Lily's voice as she said her vows and the radiant beauty of her face stayed with him forever.

"I, Lily DuCray," she vowed, "take you, Leonardo Guerra, to be my lawfully wedded husband, to have and to hold, to honor and obey, as long as we both shall live, so help me God."

Then the priest said, "I now pronounce you Man and Wife. You may kiss the bride."

The kiss lasted long and elicited hoots and catcalls at its raw passion, and they would never forget that moment.

Then the salsa band started up, singing a song Lily had comprised in the hospital, and which Leo had translated. Lily and Leo took the first dance.

El sol brilla sobre mi cabeza, desde que compartes mi cama.
Buenas cosas estan pasando, miramos Adelante y no abajo.
Me siento muy bien, tequila com lima.
Hay san risas en cada cara aqui estamos querida estes el lugar.
Yo penso que alle lugar en el sol.
Estando con mi compas y gozando.
Acompananaos y Brinda por tu novia.
Chicas bailen sacude mundo tus hombes.

The sun shines down on my head, since you've been sharing my bed.

Good things are coming around, since we're looking forward and not looking down.

I'm feeling so fine, tequila and lime.

There are smiles upon everyone's face, here we are now, honey, this is the place.

I'm thinking that I've found my Place in the Sun.

I'm hanging with my friends and having some fun.

So, join us and lift up a glass to your girl.

Girls get up and dance, honey, shake your man's world.

They finished the dance to the cheers of their friends, and Lily took the microphone, saying, "It is hard to believe the hardships Leo and I came through to be with you all here today, and I can only thank God that we survived it at all. Now it is hard to believe how wonderful life has become, and how hopeful we are for the future."

"We ask that you all join us as we pray that we can all find our Place in the Sun."

Bibliography

Bailey, David P. *Chasing the Dream: The Role of Myth in Spanish Exploration of the American West,* Museum of the West, Grand Junction, CO, 2016.

Bailey, David P. *Distant Treasures in the Mist: The Mystery of the Redoubt Site,* Museum of the West, Grand Junction, CO, 2017.

Duran, Diego. *Book of the Gods and Rites and the Ancient Calendar,* translated and edited by Fernando Horcasitas and Doris Heyden, University of Oklahoma Press, Norman, Oklahoma, 1971.

Duran, Diego. *The History of the Indies of New Spain,* translated, annotated, and with introduction by Doris Heyden. Norman: University of Oklahoma Press, 1994.

Eberhart, Perry. *Treasure Tales of the Rockies.* Athens, OH: Ohio University Press, 1969.

The GeoZone. *The Lost Spanish Mine of Culebra Peak.* Retrieved 2016, from http://www.thegeozone.com/treasure/colorado/tales/co017a.jsp

Ragsdale, Terri. *A Legend of Grand Mesa.* Grand Junction, CO: Dreamtime Press, 2010.

Waters, Stephanie. *Colorado Legends and Lore, The Phantom Fiddler, Snow Snakes, and Other Tales.* Charleston, SC: The History Press, 2014.

Made in the USA
Middletown, DE
16 September 2018